KV-374-627

The Trouble with Mojitos

ROMY SOMMER

Harper
impulse
we've got the love

Harper*Impulse* an imprint of
HarperCollins*Publishers* Ltd
77–85 Fulham Palace Road
Hammersmith, London W6 8JB

www.harpercollins.co.uk

A Paperback Original 2013

First published in Great Britain in ebook format by Harper*Impulse* 2013

Copyright © Romy Sommer 2013

Cover Images © Shutterstock.com

Romy Sommer asserts the moral right to
be identified as the author of this work

A catalogue record for this book
is available from the British Library

ISBN: 978-0-00-755976-3

This novel is entirely a work of fiction.
The names, characters and incidents portrayed in it are
the work of the author's imagination. Any resemblance to
actual persons, living or dead, events or localities is
entirely coincidental.

Automatically produced by Atomik ePublisher from Easypress

All rights reserved. No part of this publication may be
reproduced, stored in a retrieval system, or transmitted,
in any form or by any means, electronic, mechanical,
photocopying, recording or otherwise, without the prior
permission of the publishers.

To Donna, for a lifetime of friendship.

Prologue

There is a legend told by the elders of Los Pajaros of how the neighbouring island of Tortuga came to be uninhabited.

It was midsummer, at the height of the seventeenth century, when the ship first sailed into the calm waters of the natural harbour at Fredrikshafen. In those days, the town was a prosperous settlement and traders came from all corners of the Caribbean to sell sugar, spices and slaves, so a ship was not an uncommon sight. But there was something different about this ship, so that heads turned and all work along the docks ceased as the ship sailed into view.

The legends say it was a ship made of gold, encrusted with jewels, its sails made of the finest silks from the Indies. For it was a royal ship, and it carried a princess.

There was one man on the docks, though, for whom the ship's arrival was to mean more than just a sight to behold. He was a pirate captain, a hard man who'd been cast out of his homeland, a man with no heart. But when he saw the princess, fair and pale and regal where she stood in the ship's prow looking towards the island which was to be her new home, he saw the vulnerability in her face, and he loved her.

As the ship berthed beside the quay, the princess waited on its deck for her betrothed, the governor of these islands. She looked out over the busy docks and she saw a man who made her heart beat faster and her breath quicken.

By the time her betrothed came to claim her, it was too late.

As the governor led his princess away, to the golden carriage that awaited them, she turned to look back over her shoulder and her gaze met that of the dark-eyed man who'd won her heart with nothing more than a crooked smile.

The pirate winked at her.

The governor and his royal bride were to be married within the week, in a festival with more pomp and finery than the islanders had ever seen, a festival worthy of royalty. The people crowded the streets to see the show, and they got a show indeed.

For the pirate led his marauders right into the heart of the town's cathedral, and snatched the bride from before the very altar to take her back to his home on Tortuga.

The governor sent his ships in hot pursuit of the pirate ship, and the sound of their cannon balls rocked the whole island. The battle raged, fierce and terrifying, for a day and a night before silence fell at last.

Only one ship returned.

It sailed into the harbour with the grim-faced governor at the helm. Neither he nor any of his sailors ever spoke of that day again, but soon everyone on Los Pajaros knew that the governor had cast a curse on Isla Tortuga. He was from the far away land of Westerwald, a land rich in magic as well as gold, and his curse carried all the magic of his people.

From that moment on, the governor waged a war on all pirates, dedicating his life to hunting them down and killing them. And when a terrible storm ravaged Tortuga and the citizens came begging for refuge, the governor showed them no mercy and ordered them killed too.

And so the island of Tortuga was abandoned to its fate. Those fishermen who strayed too close returned with tales of the carcasses of ships lying deep in the water, and claimed they heard the death cries of the many of who died that fateful day. Gradually the sea covered over the wrecks, and a coral reef grew around them, and none but the sea turtles ever disturbed their slumber.

"But what became of the princess and her pirate captain?" the children of Los Pajaros always ask.

Their elders shrug. "No one ever knew their fate. Some say they drowned with their ship in the great battle. Some say they died in the storm, abandoned by their own people who blamed them for their ruin."

But there is one old woman, a wizened, wise woman, who tells anyone who will listen that the pirate and his princess were happy, because they lived and died together.

"And..." she leans close, her voice a rough whisper, "it is said that when the pirate and his princess return to Isla Tortuga, the curse will be broken."

Chapter One

"A mojito, please."

Kenzie sagged against the bar counter, not caring that her order sounded desperate or her body language suggested impatience. She needed alcohol, and she needed it now.

The benefit of an empty bar was that the drink came reassuringly quickly, poured from an ice cold jug ready and waiting, and complete with swizzle stick, sprig of mint and paper parasol. She ditched all of them and tossed the drink back.

"Rough day?" The dreadlocked bar tender leaned on the scarred wooden counter.

"You don't know the half of it."

"Want to talk about it?"

"Thanks, but I didn't come here to talk." She'd done enough of that all day. Talk, talk, talk, and still nothing to show for it. Now she understood how used car salesmen felt. Used.

It was enough to drive a girl to drink. Or at least to the resort's beach bar, since hitting the minibar in her hotel room was just too sad to contemplate.

She didn't drink alone. For that matter, she didn't usually drink. Not these days.

Beyond the thatched cabana, the sky flamed every shade of pink and orange imaginable as the sun set over the white sand and surf. But here inside the bar was dark, shadowy and strangely comforting after a day of white-hot heat.

"She'll have another."

She turned to the wryly amused voice, and wished she hadn't as she spotted the dark figure at the shadowy end of the long bar. Great. The resident barfly, no doubt. As if she needed another reason to hate this resort, this island, and the whole stinking Caribbean.

"I can order my own drinks, thank you."

The shadowed figure shrugged and turned his attention back to his own drink. "Suit yourself."

What was it with the men in this place? They didn't think a woman could order her own drinks, didn't think a woman could do business, wouldn't even give her the time of day. She ground her teeth, the effects of the first drink not quite enough to blur the edges of her mood. "I'd like another, please."

She ignored the deep-throated chuckle down the other end of the bar as the barman removed her glass to re-fill it.

The second drink followed the first a little more slowly, and this time she took a moment to savour the alcohol-drenched mint leaves. Now she felt better.

But she was still screwed.

Neil had known it when he sent her out here. He'd known she'd be stonewalled, he knew he'd set her an impossible task, and still he'd sent her. He'd expected her to fail. Perhaps even wanted her to fail.

There were days when her past seemed very far behind her. And then there were days like today, when it seemed she'd never escape the follies of her youth.

"Sod him!"

"That's the spirit." The stranger at the other end of the bar slid from his bar stool, out of the shadows and into the yellow

5

lamplight.

In another time and place he might have looked gorgeous, but in low-slung jeans that had seen better days, black long-sleeved tee, with hair in drastic need of a cut, several days' worth of beard, and darkly glittering eyes, he was devastating.

Pirate devastating. Bad boy devastating.

Kenzie swallowed. Double great.

This was supposed to be a family resort, for heaven's sake. Instead, the beach bar was as good as deserted, and she was alone with two strange men. Would the bartender leap to her defence if this latter day marauder made a move on her?

She doubted it. He'd probably stand back and laugh at the silly gringo girl, like everyone else she'd met over the last three days.

Though she tried hard not to notice, she was ultra-aware when the stranger came to stand beside her, leaning up against the bar close enough to touch. He didn't smell much like a barfly. In fact, he smelled damned fine, exuding raw, primal masculinity. She turned to face him, trying hard not to breathe him in.

"What do you want?" she challenged, setting her hands on her hips.

"Nothing. I just don't think it's healthy to drink alone."

"Oh really? And what exactly were *you* doing before I got here?"

His mouth quirked, on the edge of a not-quite smile. "I came here so I wouldn't have to drink alone."

He seriously needed a better pick-up line. "Good luck finding someone else to drink with, then. I don't need company."

"Are you always this friendly?"

He was smirking, damn him!

She was usually much friendlier. But since she'd sworn off bad boys for good, she didn't need this one in her face, oozing smarminess and temptation. And especially on a day like this when she'd been forcibly reminded how hanging out with the wrong sort could destroy a girl's reputation.

There was even a moment this afternoon she'd contemplated

changing her name and starting fresh somewhere else. Perhaps across the Atlantic, because England just seemed to be getting smaller with every passing year.

She turned back to the bartender. "Where is everyone, anyway? I thought this resort was near capacity."

Again it wasn't the bartender who answered. "It's karaoke night in the main hotel bar." Which would explain the blaring 80s music she'd heard on her way past reception.

"You don't want to join them?" She barely caught the mockery beneath her drinking companion's words.

She wrinkled her nose. "I'm not really into karaoke, thanks."

"So you're here to get drunk then. Join the club." He raised his glass to her. Rum and cola. A pirate's drink. How unimaginative.

"I never get drunk. I just had a tough day."

"What was so tough about it – too much snorkelling, sailing and lying on the beach?" This time the mocking tone was impossible to miss.

She straightened her shoulders. "I'm here to work, not play."

"Pity." He glanced down over her attire, taking in the crumpled white tee, khaki cargo pants and dusty hiking boots. "You don't look dressed for work. What is it you do?"

"I'm a location scout for a film company that wants to shoot a feature here on the island." Or rather a film company that wanted to shoot somewhere in the Caribbean. There were other scouts out on other islands. She'd only been thrown this job as a bone to her best friend, who'd practically begged for Kenzie to be given a chance.

The pirate's gaze swept over her again with the same sardonic look she'd got from the harbour master, the clerk at the mayor's office, and that officious jerk at Environmental Services. "A film shoot. Sounds like fun."

Except he didn't sound at all thrilled. He sounded bored. The same way she was starting to feel. Just three days ago, she'd been so psyched for this job that she'd practically bounced off the plane.

Warm sun, wide blue sky, palm trees, and the chance to finally prove her worth – what wasn't there to like about Los Pajaros?

A lot it seemed.

She really needed to recapture her enthusiasm. Perhaps if she were more passionate, she'd be able to convince someone... anyone...to give this film a shot. To give *her* a shot.

She injected as much excitement into her voice as she could muster. "It's kind of *Pirates of the Caribbean* meets *Lost*. With a bit of comedy thrown in."

Not that she'd read the script, of course. That was classified. All she'd needed to know was the list of locations the director wanted and how much the producer was willing to pay for them. Easy, right?

It should have been. She'd fixed locations for dozens of shoots, usually the kind that had nothing more than goodwill to pay with. Now she had a big studio movie, a Hollywood director to impress and a budget to die for, and she couldn't get a foot in the door. What was wrong with this place?

The pirate's blistering, dark gaze raked over her. "So what does a location scout do?"

"Mostly I take pictures and send them back to the director. If he likes what he sees, then I negotiate permission for the crew to film there."

"Does your director like what he's seen so far?"

And that was where her problems began. She hadn't sent a thing yet. Not anything the director could use, anyway. She had no doubt the scouts who'd been sent to the Virgin Islands and Bahamas were doing way better.

"I hired a charter boat, but the skipper only took me to all the usual tourist spots, and they're completely useless for our needs. Either too small, or too rocky, or too busy. I'm looking for a bay big enough to hold a pirate ship, and a long stretch of white beach with no sign of human habitation – and preferably a handy bit of tropical forest that isn't too dense for us to shoot in."

8

She rubbed the back of her neck. "According to Google Earth, there are a few uninhabited islands not far from Los Pajaros, but the skipper refused to take me to any of them without a permit. The clerk at the harbour master's refused to give me the permit without a letter from the Environmental Services office, who refused to give me a letter without the governor's permission."

"The governor's role is purely titular. He wouldn't be much help."

"I gathered. His office sent me to the mayor and he's almost impossible to get in to see. I waited for the entire afternoon. Do you know the mayor's waiting room doesn't even have air conditioning! How can the mayor's office not have air conditioning?"

"Depends which waiting room you're in." Her pirate smiled for the first time, but there was still a twist of mockery in the way his mouth curved. "There are two, and only one gets you an audience."

She'd suspected that officious secretary wanted to get rid of her. Even the women of Los Pajaros had it in for her. She recognised the run around when she saw it, but she wasn't going to be so easy to get rid of.

He waved his now empty glass at the bartender. "Your boss doesn't like you much, does he?"

"How can you tell?"

"Because he couldn't have sent a worse person to do the job."

Kenzie bristled. "I'm really good at what I do!"

"How old are you...twenty two?"

She pulled her shoulders straight and thrust her head high. "*Thirty* two."

He shrugged. "No offence, sweetheart, but one, you're a woman. Two, you look like a kid fresh out of high school. And three, you're not from around here. This is a tight-knit community and wary of strangers. If your boss had done his homework, he'd have sent a man. Preferably a man with Caribbean connections."

That figured. Neil always did his homework, so he'd known she was all wrong for the job and he'd sent her anyway. He made no secret he thought she was nothing more than a party girl playing at being a location scout.

The face didn't help. Baby face genes were more a curse than anyone realised.

So Neil had given the plum pickings of the Caribbean to the other scouts and sent her off to chase the long shot, the backwater island group that had never hosted a big film shoot before. She was sure the other scouts weren't getting the same run around.

Still, until today, she'd been convinced she could prove him wrong. That feeling she'd had ever since she could remember that something amazing was just around the corner, seemed stronger than ever.

Gran had always said she had good instincts, and from the moment she'd seen the satellite images of these islands, Kenzie's instincts had been screaming at her.

She sighed and closed her eyes. Perhaps her instincts were lying. It wouldn't be the first time. And after ten years of trying one job after another and never finding that dream, her usual optimism was starting to take a beating.

What did Gran know, anyhow? The last time Kenzie had visited the nursing home, Gran hadn't even recognised her.

She didn't argue when the bartender refilled her mojito glass. She lifted it in a toast to her drinking companion. "Sod them all."

He raised his drink and grinned. "Sod them all."

They drank in silence, and when she was done, Kenzie pushed her glass away. Three mojitos on an empty stomach was her limit for one day.

She needed to regroup. She needed a back up plan.

After all, she'd been in the film business long enough now to know that nothing ever went according to plan the first time round. There was always a Plan B. Or C or D. And somehow everything always worked out in the end.

She would make it. She was destined for great things, and this movie would be the beginning. She'd start with some positive thinking and an attitude adjustment.

Plastering on her best 'I just know you're gonna love me' smile, she held out her hand. "I'm Mackenzie Cole. My friends call me Kenzie."

He gave her outstretched hand a perfunctory shake. "Rik."

"You have a surname?"

"None that matters."

She rolled her eyes. "So Rik, what do you do for a living?"

"Nothing much."

Hmm. So he was going to play the Mystery Man. She squinted suspiciously at him. "You're not some trust fund baby out for a good time, are you?"

"Do I look like I'm having a good time?" The mockery was back in his eyes, but this time she guessed it was aimed more at himself than at her.

She shrugged. Whatever shadows he carried, she wanted no part of them. She was done with men who needed fixing. Besides, her plane ticket was booked for three days from now. That wasn't enough time to fix whatever was broken with Rik My-Name-Doesn't-Matter, even if she hadn't already had her fill of bad boys.

She and Lee had sworn a vow – from now on they were dating nice men only. Gentlemen. The kind who didn't bring trouble in their wake. Her BFF would kill her if she weakened barely two weeks in.

So back to work. She toyed with her glass. "How does a girl with no local connections and a burning need to be heard get an audience with the mayor?" It was a rhetorical question. She didn't really expect an answer from either the latter day pirate or the bartender.

She should have known she'd get one anyway.

"You don't. You go home and tell your boss not to send a girl to do a man's job."

Between one breath and the next, the red haze descended, staining her vision with anger. She slammed her hands down on the bar counter. "I *can't* and I *won't* go back a failure!"

Rik eyed the little firecracker over the rim of his glass and grinned. She was certainly living up to the flaming colour of her hair. He admired her spirit, misguided as it was.

"If you're not going to do the sensible thing and drop it, then you'll need an introduction. Someone who knows the mayor and can get you in the door. On this island, you convince the mayor, you convince everyone else."

"Great. So is there anyone you know who can open the mayor's door for me?"

Silence. The bartender, bored by the conversation, had drifted away to re-fill the pretzel bowls, and Rik suddenly found something very interesting in the bottom of his glass.

He could do it. Perhaps even should do it.

Except he hadn't felt very much like doing anything for anyone in a very long time. Sod them all, indeed.

His glass was empty. He couldn't even remember drinking that last drink, so the alcohol must be starting to do its job at last. But it hadn't numbed him enough yet. He could still feel the summons burning a hole in his pocket.

He waved his empty glass at the bartender. "Why don't you just give up?" he asked, finally catching the barman's eye.

"Because things always work out in the end."

He rolled his eyes. What kind of naivety was that? Clearly, she'd lived a very sheltered life if she believed persistence was all you needed to get what you want. Sometimes life just kicked you in the nuts for no damn good reason. "I suppose I could."

"Could what?"

Not just naive, but slow on the uptake too. "I could introduce you to the mayor."

"You? I thought you had to have connections to get anything done here. You're not from around here, are you?"

"No."

She pursed her lips, clearly wanting a more elaborate explanation. She'd have to learn to live with disappointment. If there was one thing he'd learned in this new life that had been forced on him, it was that he didn't owe anyone anything. And that included explanations.

"So how do you propose to introduce me to the mayor?"

She didn't give up, did she? Like a mosquito buzzing in a room, tenacious and annoying. But at least the mosquito's buzz was insistent enough to drive out the awareness of other pains.

He sighed. "I'll drive you there in the morning, ask to see him. After that, the ball's in your court."

"That simple?" Kenzie's eyes narrowed.

"That simple." His glass seemed to have a hole in the bottom. It was already empty. Or had the barman not yet re-filled it? The mosquito buzz seemed louder now.

"If I take you to see the mayor, what do I get in return?" Rik asked, not looking at her.

"I have money," she said. "If that's what you want."

He looked at her then, up and down the fragile frame encased in non-branded department store clothing. There was no way she had the kind of money that would mean anything to him. And since he not only had his inheritance, but also the rather handsome payment he'd been given to disappear, money was the last thing he needed.

"Not money."

The blood ran to the surface of her near translucent skin. "I'm not giving you *that*."

He laughed, a mirthless, rusty sound, even to his own ears. "I sure as hell don't need to bribe you for sex either, honey."

Though he was sure sex with her would be fun, he'd never needed to bribe anyone for anything. Everything he'd ever wanted had been handed to him on a platter, including women.

But no matter how attractive the idea was, he wasn't in any fit state for that now. Tonight it wasn't sex he wanted, but oblivion.

"Keep my car keys safe for me until the morning." He removed the keys from the back pocket of his jeans and slid them onto the bar counter between them.

"That's it?" She lifted an eyebrow. She had the most piercing blue eyes he'd ever seen, as clear as the water in the bay where he swam every day. "How do I get them back to you?"

"I'll meet you in the hotel reception at ten."

"How can I be sure you'll be there?"

He rubbed a hand over his eyes. "Because you have my keys." And besides, he'd had more entertainment in the last half hour than he'd had since he arrived in Los Pajaros. That had to be worth a little effort in return. "I'll be there."

She hesitated a moment before she took the keys and hopped off her bar stool. "In which case, I need to get my beauty sleep."

"Hey Pollyanna..." She was halfway out of the bar when he called after her. "You might want to wear a dress. A short skirt will get you much further with the mayor than your current ensemble."

"I don't own a dress."

"You could make a stop in the resort boutique first thing in the morning."

She shook her head and kept on walking, and with a chuckle he turned back to the barman to order another drink.

When it arrived, he stuck Kenzie's discarded swizzle stick and umbrella into the glass. "Happy birthday to me." He downed the drink in one long gulp.

Chapter Two

@KenzieCole101: Sheesh I'm tired. See you in 8 hours world.

@LeeHill: What's up Mac? I'm not even asleep yet and I'm 5 hours ahead.

@KenzieCole101: You know I'm useless without a full night's sleep.

Kenzie woke to the insistent ringing of a phone. Not the chirpy tone of her mobile, but a shrill tring-tring. The room was still dark.

She pushed her long fringe out of her eyes and groped for the hotel phone on the bedside table. "Hello?"

"Miss Cole? This is the night manager. We require your urgent assistance at the beach bar please."

What the…? "What time is it?"

"It's a little after 1am."

He must have the wrong person. Why on earth would she be needed in a bar in the middle of the night? "You have the wrong room." Her voice was still scratchy with sleep.

"You're not Miss Cole?" The man's voice rose in anxiety.

"I am, but I'm sure you have the wrong person."

The manager cleared his throat. "It's about your young man."

What young man?

Oh heavens, he had to mean Rik. What had he done? A tremor of ice ran down her spine and brought her fully awake. But he couldn't have gone anywhere – she still had his car keys.

"Is he okay?" she asked, struggling upwards and fumbling for the light switch.

"He's passed out." And the manager sounded very unimpressed.

She rubbed her eyes. "I'll be right down."

She pulled on a sweatshirt and jogging bottoms, tied her hair back in a ponytail, and slid her feet into the espadrilles she'd bought on her first day in Los Pajaros in celebration of having arrived in the tropics. Then she headed downstairs.

Why was she always dragged into other people's shit? She really had to learn to be less trusting of people. She should have taken one look at that rugged face and those glittering eyes and run as far away and as fast as she could.

But no…she always had to give people the benefit of the doubt. And now here she was, in the dead of night, about to take on someone else's problems yet again.

The 80s music had long since ceased and the reception lights were on low. But outside the path that meandered between swimming pools and luscious gardens was as brightly lit as Piccadilly Circus on a hot summer's night.

The thatched bar lay right at the end of the path, where the grassy lawn met the sandy beach. It didn't look much different than when she'd been there earlier in the evening, a little darker, but still deserted and still full of shadows.

The dreadlocked barman had emerged from behind his bar and was now huddled over a figure sprawled face down across one of the rough wooden tables. Beside him stood a harassed looking young man in a wrinkled white suit who had to be the manager.

"What's the problem?" she asked in her most cheerful voice.

The manager turned, his face transforming from aggrieved to

16

relieved in an instant. Kenzie wished she felt the same, but instead her heart hit the bottom of her espadrilles.

"We need to get him out of here," the manager said, huffing as he tried to lift Rik's dead weight. "Where does he need to go?"

"How the hell should I know?" Kenzie frowned at the two men.

"He gave you his car keys," the barman pointed out.

"Yes. He asked me to keep them until the morning so he wouldn't drive anywhere in this state." She turned to the manager. "Surely you must know which room he's in."

The manager stiffened, righteous indignation written all over him. "He's not a guest of this hotel."

It just kept on coming.

"Maybe there's something in his car that will tell us where he belongs?" she suggested. "Then perhaps we can call a cab and send him home."

"We can't leave him here while we look," the manager said. "What if he wakes up and wanders into the sea, or one of the pools? I don't want to be responsible for that."

Neither did she. "Okay, we'll have to take him with us to the main building."

It took both men to lift Rik off the table. Then, with his arms looped around their shoulders, they began the shuffle back along the brightly lit path. The trip took at least three times as long as it had taken Kenzie on the way down. Impatient to get rid of the lot of them and back to the comfort of her king-size bed, she lengthened her strides and hurried ahead, fingering the car keys in her pocket.

She had no idea how she was going to identify which car she was looking for. This could take all night.

But when she reached the guest car park, it wasn't too hard to work out which car was Rik's. The car park was packed full of vehicles that were obviously rentals – all but one, a sleek black Lamborghini.

Doing 'Nothing much' clearly paid a lot of money. Perhaps he really was a pirate. Or a drug smuggler. What if she found packages of cocaine stashed beneath the seats?

With her heart knocking against her ribs, Kenzie scoured the car for clues. Nothing. Not a driver's licence, no scraps of paper – not even a bank bag of marijuana. Relieved by the last but frustrated by the first, she sat down in the passenger seat and racked her brains.

Who was this man? A local, a guest at another hotel? His accent was indistinct. There'd been a hint of something European, but equally he spoke as if he'd learned his English at Eton or Harrow.

She rubbed her forehead. Was anyone missing him?

She jumped as a shadow moved beside her.

"Found anything?" the manager asked, bending down into view.

She shook her head. "Nothing. Did you check if he had any ID on him, or credit cards?"

"Of course. The only thing in his wallet was cash."

What kind of man drove a fancy sports car but didn't even have a credit card? In her experience, wealthy people always had plastic of the platinum variety, and weren't afraid to use it.

Unless her pirate needed to conceal his identity?

Perhaps he was an assassin. Or a stockbroker caught embezzling funds who was now on the run from the law.

She climbed out the car and slammed the door shut. "There's only one thing to do then."

"What?"

"You'll have to put him up in a room for the rest of the night."

The manager drew up his thin shoulders, offended. "We don't just give out rooms to everyone who gets drunk in this hotel. I'll have to call the police."

Kenzie rubbed her temple where an ache had begun to bloom. If Rik spent the night in a police cell, what were the chances he'd be able to take her to the mayor's office any time soon? Assuming of course that hadn't all been a big fat lie.

She squeezed her eyes shut. He'd seemed genuine enough when he offered. Unwilling, but genuine.

Damn him. She needed the mayor's permission so she could do her bloody job and get off this island and carry on with the rest of her life. Which meant she needed him.

"Fine," she snapped. "He can sleep in my room."

There was a sofa. And Rik was so out of it, he'd never even notice he was way too tall for it.

Back in the hotel lobby, Rik lay on a plush banquette, the barman hovering wearily nearby. On the plus side, and unlike Brett, her most recent and completely unlamented ex, Rik neither snored nor drooled in this state.

As the two now red-faced hotel employees manhandled him into the lift, Rik surfaced long enough to mumble "sod them all" before sinking back against the glass wall.

Sod you too, Kenzie thought. *And Neil, for sending me into this mess.* Though in all fairness, she couldn't blame the film's producer. She'd wanted this job. Had begged for it.

As noiselessly as they could, they half-carried, half-dragged Rik down the corridor to her room and she opened the door with her key card.

"On the sofa," she instructed the men, and they dumped Rik unceremoniously down.

"Are you sure I shouldn't call the police?" the manager asked, eyeing Rik's prostrate form.

"Absolutely not," she said, in the crispest, most professional voice she could muster at this time of night. Or this time of morning.

The barman and manager couldn't get out fast enough, and Kenzie didn't stop them. She latched the door behind them and sagged against it.

There had to be worse ways to spend a Friday night, although nothing sprang to mind.

Her gaze fell on Rik, twisted uncomfortably on the sofa. Tough shit. Served him right if he woke with a sore back as well as a sore head.

It was only when she'd undressed and climbed into bed that

she noticed the piece of paper sticking out the pocket of Rik's jeans. The manager clearly hadn't done a particularly thorough job of searching him.

She shouldn't bother. She should switch out the light, pull the covers over her head, and get back to sleep.

But that scrap of paper gnawed at her. What if it could tell her who Rik was and where he belonged?

Curiosity won. She padded across the room and eased it out of his pocket, trying hard not to look an inch to the left at the bulge in his jeans. Rik mumbled and rolled over, and she jumped back.

But he didn't wake.

The paper was a single page, creased as though it had been crumpled in anger then smoothed out again. She really shouldn't unfold it. She should put it back. It was none of her business...

Oh what the hell...

She unfolded the paper. A letter. No address, just a barely visible embossed logo in the top left hand corner, in the same ivory colour as the paper itself. The note was hand-written in a large, old-fashioned hand, very neat, and dated several weeks ago.

Rik – you've been a pain to track down. No more hiding - we need to talk. I expect you at my engagement party and I'm not taking 'no' for an answer. I'll owe you big. Max

Nothing there to give any hint of who Rik was, yet something tugged at the edge of her memory, just out of reach. She moved to the bedside table and sat on the edge of the bed, holding the letter to the light. The paper was thinner than regular office paper, expensive, and the logo caught the light. Not a logo after all but an heraldic crest, a dragon framed by climbing roses. The memory nudged harder. She'd seen it before, and recently.

Think, think.

The mayor's waiting room! She'd spent the better part of the afternoon staring at this shield, only it had been in full colour, above the obligatory portrait of the governor hanging on the wall. It was the emblem of Westerwald, the nation that owned this southern Caribbean archipelago.

The same nation that had been in the tabloids a great deal lately.

Fredrik and Maximilian... she slapped her forehead. She'd never have recognised him with the beard and overlong hair, but it had to be... She had a prince on the sofa in her hotel room! A disinherited prince, to be sure, but that hardly mattered.

A *missing* disinherited prince. She wondered what the tabloids would pay for news of his whereabouts. Nope, not going there. There was no amount of money in the world that would induce her to throw someone into that rapacious spotlight. Been there, done that, and burned the tee shirt.

She perched on the edge of her bed and considered the letter. Just last week she'd sat in the Soho production office and flicked through a magazine article on the recently announced royal nuptials in Westerwald. There'd been a great deal made about the guest list for the upcoming engagement party, a party Rik was clearly expected to attend.

How she'd love to have been a fly on the wall during that confrontation!

No wonder Rik had drunk himself comatose. The thought of going back to the country that had thrown him out, to face the brother who'd succeeded him, perhaps even the mother who'd passed him off as another man's child, all under the glare of the paparazzi cameras... she'd have got drunk too.

Kenzie set the letter down and took a hard look at him.

Prince Fredrik von Waldburg of Westerwald.

There'd been a picture of him with the article. She remembered it clearly, since she'd stopped for a long look. He'd been dressed in a suit and tie, clean-shaven and conservative, but there'd been a suggestion of ruggedness that had appealed to her even then.

He'd had a glossy blonde on his arm in the picture, a girlfriend with a title to match the perfect looks and catwalk evening gown.

What had happened to her? She'd probably gone the way of his inheritance.

Kenzie set the letter down on the bed and stared at her unwelcome visitor. At least he hadn't lied about being able to introduce her to the mayor. Even disinherited, he probably had the kind of connections that could open a lot of doors for her.

Her heart skittered with excitement. She'd known she was on the verge of something big. Neil had sent her here to fail. But with Rik's help, she could get the job done and prove to him, and to herself, that she was more than just the poor choices she'd made a decade ago.

You see. Things always work out in the end.

Rik lay on his stomach, one leg over the arm of the sofa, the other trailing on the floor. One arm hung at an odd angle and his face was crushed into the cushions. He was going to have an interesting pattern on his face when he woke.

Oh heavens – when he woke...!

What the hell was she going to say? *Good morning, your highness, would you like your pillows fluffed?*

Stuff that. She'd had enough of that with the second in her long line of exes. Charlie had expected her to bow to his every whim because he had money and a title, and she'd been so awed by the world he'd introduced her to that she'd done it. She'd gone along with every stupid, hare-brained scheme of his, until she'd been hung out to dry in full public view. The memory rose like bile in her throat. Never again!

It seemed all these rich boys were the same; too much money and nothing better to do with their time than party and get wasted. Though to be fair, those with very little money still had the same tendency, as Brett had proved.

It had all seemed so glam when she'd been in her heady twenties, young and impressionable, but she was older and wiser now. There was nothing glamorous about having a man passed out on one's sofa, no matter who he was.

Tomorrow she'd pretend she knew nothing more than what Rik had told her. He could carry on playing Mystery Man, for all she cared. She wasn't going to bow and scrape, and she sure as hell wasn't going to let herself be seduced. She was just one bad relationship away from getting thirty cats and calling it quits with men.

She folded up the letter and crossed the room to slide it back into his pocket. Which was definitely not as easy as pulling it out had been.

Job done, she surveyed the sleeping beauty on her sofa. There was a hint of vulnerability in his face that definitely wasn't there when he was awake. It tugged at something inside her, and she swallowed hard. No, she wasn't going to try to fix this one. She had to have learned that lesson by now, right?

But she couldn't in good conscience leave a prince to sleep like a pretzel on the sofa, no matter how much of a pain in the butt he was, or how much he deserved it.

The first and easiest thing she could do for him was to remove his shoes. She unlaced his trainers, braced her knees on the edge of the sofa, and pulled. His shoe slid off, quicker than she expected, the momentum driving her straight onto him, with her knee in his groin.

"Ooph." Rik's eyes fluttered, and her heart stopped beating.

His eyelids settled, and she laid a hand over her heart and started to breathe again. He was seriously out of it not to be woken by *that*.

With much more care, she removed his other trainer, then stood back to survey the scene.

She'd move him to the bed, and she'd take the sofa. She had more chance of fitting on it anyway. Who knew there'd be a perk to being only five foot three?

But getting him onto the bed was an altogether different matter. It had taken two grown men to get him to her room, so how the hell was she going to get him from the sofa to the bed on her own?

She started by wrestling the sofa closer to the bed.

Deep breath in and shove. Deep breath in and shove.

23

Sweat beaded on her forehead as the sofa inched slowly forwards until, with a jolt, it connected with the side of the bed.

Great. Now what?

She had to climb over the back of the sofa to roll Rik onto the bed. Except he didn't want to roll. He snuggled back into the sofa cushions.

"Give me a break!"

Since she'd come this far, there was no going back. She wrapped her arms around his torso and heaved. He wasn't a small man and in sleep he was damned heavy and uncooperative. He was also rather buff. She couldn't help but notice the firmness of muscle beneath that long black tee. She'd bet anything he had a fine six-pack. For half a second she was tempted to strip off his shirt for a peek. Surely the vow she and Lee had sworn didn't preclude looking?

No, a promise was a promise.

Besides, she was now hot and sweaty, in spite of the air-con, and wrestling him out of his clothes just wasn't worth the effort, so she discarded the idea as quickly as it formed. She'd have to be satisfied with having copped a feel.

Rik now lay on the very edge of the bed. She climbed over him to kneel on his other side. One last heave and he'd be safe and comfortable and she could get to sleep herself.

She wrapped her arms around him, and he moaned. Not the same sound he'd made before, but a satisfied purr. Oh heaven help her! If he woke now, there was no way she could explain why she had him in her bed, in a very intimate and compromising position.

She half-pulled, half-rolled with him.

The good news was that she managed to get him away from the edge of the bed. The bad news? She was now pinned underneath him.

And yes, that was definitely a very fine six-pack beneath the shirt. Perhaps even an eight-pack.

Up this close, the smell of rum was more pronounced. On any

other man it would have been a complete turn-off. On Rik it just added to the pirate allure.

But he was heavy, and this was neither the right time nor place to get turned on. And most certainly not the right man. She was looking for a *nice* man, remember? Or better yet, no man at all. Not until she could stand tall, with her head high and say 'Look at me: I'm a success!'

She wedged her hands against his torso and shoved with all her strength. Rik rolled off her, and she lay breathless, needing a moment to regroup.

Yay! He was now safely on her king-size bed, cuddling into the pillow where she'd slept in such blissful ignorance barely an hour ago.

@KenzieCole101: I need a cold shower.

Chapter Three

@LeeHill: @KenzieCole101 What's up chica? Heat keeping you awake?

@KenzieCole101: @LeeHill Something like that. But I'm behaving. Promise!

Light filtered through Rik's eyelids and he groaned into his pillow. Whoever had stuck his head in a vice grip then twisted it deserved to die. He'd see to it personally. Just as soon as he could lift his head off the pillow to see who it was.

"Time to wake up, Sleeping Beauty."

The voice was annoyingly perky and not one he recognised. Probably a new housemaid. Where was Robert? It was usually his valet who brought his coffee and the morning papers.

With herculean effort he lifted one eyelid.

Ouch, the light was bright.

He didn't recognise her face either. And the housemaids didn't usually wear jeans. He squeezed his eyes shut again, but that was worse. Now the room reeled about him.

It wasn't a sensation he was used to, but in a sickening instant he knew he was neither dreaming nor ill. He was hungover. And there wasn't going to be any valet or housemaid, because they belonged to a life that wasn't his anymore.

"Here drink this. It'll make you feel better."

Nothing could do that. He'd already tried. Neither time nor distance nor drink could dull the constant ache.

He prised his eyes open. "What is it?"

"A special concoction the concierge cooked up. He swears on his grandmother's grave it works miracles."

Rik hoped so. Gingerly, he levered himself up on his elbow and took the glass of foaming green liquid from her outstretched hand. "What's in it?"

She shrugged. "Local herbs or something."

Local herbs – who was she kidding? "Isn't it bad enough you got me drunk? Now you want to get me stoned too?"

"I didn't get you drunk. You did that all on your own. And I don't want you stoned either. I want you sober and out of my bed so I can get to work."

The drink tasted surprisingly minty and though the first sip made him gag, he managed to drink it all down.

"There's a good boy. Ready to get up now?"

"Ask me in another hour." He shut his eyes and sagged back into the pillow's softness. At least the room seemed to have stopped spinning about him. A miracle indeed.

She ripped the duvet off him. "Oh no, you don't! It's already ten o'clock and the day is wasting away."

He pulled the duvet back. "Great, go and enjoy it," he mumbled into the pillow. "I'll stay here and sleep it off. You won't even know I'm here."

"You're taking me to see the mayor."

Why would he do that? He didn't want to think, didn't want to remember, but gradually the memories formed anyway...the resort bar, chosen because there were few locals there and little chance he'd be recognised...the pretty firecracker who'd made him smile... the summons from his brother...

His whole damned useless life where one day dragged into

another.

He forced himself off the pillows and sat up.

The room wasn't as bright as it first appeared. Wooden shutters shielded the worst of the infernal sunshine. It leaked through the slats, casting moving patterns on the bed that made his stomach swirl.

His gaze shifted back to the redhead. No, not red... more ginger. She wore it tied back in a loose ponytail, just as she had last night. Her eyes were too big for her face, her nose pert and slightly upturned, and her skin...he'd never understood the term 'porcelain skin' until now. The dusting of freckles stood out against the delicate paleness.

Kenzie, she'd called herself. What kind of a name was that?

"You look tired," he observed.

She pursed her lips. "I wonder why?"

Her retort was too tart for him to have kept her awake in the most pleasurable of ways. So at least he hadn't missed any fun stuff. "How did I get here? Last I remember I was celebrating alone in the beach bar."

"Didn't look like much of a celebration. The night manager and barman carried you up here. It was either that or jail."

"In which case, I thank you. You have a kind heart."

She didn't seem to like the compliment. Her eyes spat blue flame. "I didn't do it for you."

"Ah yes, I promised you an introduction to the mayor. You didn't take my advice though. Didn't the hotel boutique have a dress?"

Although her jeans were a snug fit so they might do the job too. They were certainly making his mouth dry. Or maybe that was just thirst.

"I was a tad preoccupied this morning." She pursed her lips again, and he found his gaze drawn to her mouth. Against his will, he licked his own lips.

She blushed, her pale skin lighting up as the heat spread. Then she dropped her gaze and rose from the bed. "Now you're finally awake, take a shower, and I'll order you some breakfast."

"I'll have toast, plain, and I like my coffee black and sweet."

Kenzie arched an eyebrow. "Anything else you'd like?" He almost heard the sarcastic *Your Highness* she bit back. He swallowed bitter laughter. She had no idea how close to the truth she was. Or how far.

While she stalked off to call room service, he slipped into the bathroom. The shower's temperature was set on cold, and by the time he'd managed to crank up the heat, he was well and truly awake. He was also starving.

He didn't have much experience of hangovers but he was pretty sure this level of alertness was unusual. Weren't people supposed to throw up after they'd been drunk? He couldn't remember being sick. The concierge's grandmother could rest peacefully in her grave. Perhaps he should finance the concierge in a little sideline herbal remedy business.

Rik discarded the idea as quickly as he'd discarded every other Plan B he'd come up with these last few months. There wasn't a lot that an ex-prince could do without seeming like a loser or just plain desperate. Which he was. There was also only so much paradise one man could take. If he didn't find something soon to fill his days he was going to go insane.

But at least he still had his dignity – as long as the girl in the other room never got wind of who he was. A sordid night in a woman's hotel room was exactly the kind of lurid headline he didn't need.

Like mother, like son. He could picture it already.

He towelled himself dry, dressed in his jeans, and emerged from the bathroom just as the room service waiter rolled in a trolley of pastries and steaming coffee. His stomach turned over, in a good way this time.

Kenzie had her back to him. She signed for the meal, closed the door behind the waiter, and turned.

She coughed.

"Please put your shirt back on." Her voice sounded strangled.

"Do I offend your modesty?" he asked, feeling an insane urge to grin at her reaction.

She shook her head and swallowed again. "You have tattoos."

"No, really? How did that happen?" He looked down at himself, eyes wide in mock shock.

She frowned.

"You don't like tattoos?"

"I love tattoos." She turned away again, fussing over the trolley and pouring coffee.

This time he grinned. And didn't bother putting his shirt back on.

"Those tattoos aren't new," she said as she handed him a cup of coffee, careful not to look at him.

"No, they're not." They'd been his one and only form of rebellion, done right here in the islands on a holiday a couple of years ago. He'd had to be careful after that to always keep his shoulders and upper arms covered. It wouldn't do for the heir to a European throne to be seen sporting tattoos. Not even his parents had known they existed.

Now that he was free to do as he pleased he still kept them covered. They mocked him. The dragon of Westerwald that snaked across his shoulder blades and down his arms. The emblem of a nation he didn't belong to. Had never belonged to, it turned out, though it was the only home he'd ever known.

These were tattoos that no person but he and the artist had ever laid eyes on before today. Kenzie had no idea how privileged she was. He could only blame the lapse on last night's over-indulgence.

He set down his undrunk coffee and pulled his long-sleeved shirt back on over his head. "You can look again now."

She cast a furtive glance his way, long enough for him to catch the heated flush rising up her cheeks again. Interesting. So she had a serious thing for men with tattoos. And she didn't want to.

He was sure he could change her mind.

Now where had that thought come from? He'd never been a

seducer of women. In his old life he'd had a girlfriend for over a year and barely tried for more than a polite goodnight kiss. Teresa hadn't made his blood boil, and that's exactly why he'd liked her. She'd been cool, calm and rational. She'd have made the perfect Archduchess. She would never have done anything sordid, would never have created a scandal.

She probably wouldn't have approved of his tattoos either.

Kenzie was everything Teresa wasn't. She wasn't cool and collected. She wasn't a style icon. And her emotions were far too easy to read. In spite of the vulnerable eyes and heart-shaped face, sensuality smouldered beneath the surface. Emotional, sexy, complicated... she was everything he'd avoided in his old life.

She was everything he no longer needed to avoid.

He found himself grinning again. It felt good to smile. Strange, but good.

"Are you going to stand there all day, or are you going to drink your coffee so we can get moving?" she asked impatiently, perching on the edge of the sofa.

Was she always this bossy or was it just his charm that brought out her better side?

"Yes ma'am." He gulped down the coffee, grabbed a slice of toast, and sat beside her on the sofa. Since he'd woken in the bed, she must have slept here last night, judging by the blankets and pillows piled at one end. She could have made him sleep on the sofa. However much she chose to deny it, Kenzie had a kind heart.

"Aren't you going to eat?" he asked.

"I did. While you were still snoring."

"I don't snore."

She smiled, and it was an impish look. Forget smouldering sensuality. He'd guess she could be a downright bad girl if she wanted to be.

He set down his empty coffee cup, grabbed a cheese croissant from the basket and stood. "Where are my car keys? Let's roll."

She shook her head. "You're not driving. I don't trust you."

31

It wasn't just his driving. There was something in the rapid shuttering of her expression that told him exactly what she thought: it was *him* she didn't trust.

It was a moment before he realised his mouth had dropped open. No one, ever, had thought him untrustworthy. And no one had ever looked at him the way Kenzie just had – as if he were a bug squashed beneath her shoe. Nope, no matter how attractive she found him, she didn't like him.

He closed his mouth and followed her out into the corridor. The sickening feeling of disorientation was back in full force, and the unusual urge to grin deserted him.

***

The magical potion had definitely worn off. Rik clutched his head as Kenzie's compact rental car bumped over the potholed road into town. "Could you possibly try not to hit every single one?" he groaned.

The look Kenzie cast him was beyond withering. "Are all the roads on the island like this one?"

"No. Most are worse."

Only one tarred road circled the island, connecting the tourist resorts with the main town. Inland, where only the most adventurous visitors ventured, the roads were nothing but dirt.

She swerved to avoid the next major pothole, which was even worse than bumping through it. Rik hung onto the car door, feeling more than a little green. And she hadn't trusted *him* to drive?

"You're not booked into the hotel," she said, keeping her eyes on the road. "Do you live here on Los Pajaros?"

"Something like that."

He didn't need to see her to know she had rolled her eyes. "You're not good with small talk, are you?"

He was a master at small talk, had been trained in the art from the time he learned to talk. Along with many other skills that were all but useless now.

He shrugged and looked back out the window. On their right the sea flashed silver and inviting through the dense foliage that separated the road from the beach.

The undergrowth grew thinner, and the simple wooden dwellings clustered along the road grew more numerous. Then they crested the final rise and Fredrikshafen lay below them, a small town of broad avenues and colourful buildings.

Beyond the jumble of buildings lay the wide harbour. A vast passenger liner, winking white in the sunlight, dominated the largest of the piers that jutted out into the bay. Colour and vibrancy and light dazzled their eyes.

Kenzie sucked in a breath.

"It's a beautiful view, isn't it?" he asked, managing a grin now that the ordeal of the drive was behind them.

She nodded. "It's growing on me."

The place was growing on him too. He'd come to Los Pajaros because he had nowhere else to go. There could be worse places to lose oneself.

The mayor's office was housed in a white colonial building on an esplanade lined with scraggy palms that overlooked the harbour. Kenzie circled the block until she found a parking space and finally turned to Rik. "You sure you're up for this?"

She wasn't just asking how his hangover was doing. She wanted to know if he could really help her. This was his last chance to back out.

But he didn't ever back out. No matter how much he wanted to run away and hide. *We never back down from unpleasant tasks*, his father had often said. *We face them with our heads high and our hearts strong.* He flinched.

"My headache's back. Thanks for asking." He unclicked the seatbelt and ignored her frown.

Head high. He hadn't been doing a lot of that lately.

Kenzie followed him through the doors that stood open into a double volume courtyard fringed by potted palms. A military guard, sweating in his uniform, waved them past the security desk with nothing more than a curious look. Everything in the space was white, or had once been, and streaked with strips of light that fell through the high windows over the majestic staircase rising up before them.

The ground floor offices seemed deserted, though he could hear the distant murmur of voices.

Rik took the stairs two at a time, not waiting for Kenzie to follow. The sooner he got her in to see the mayor, the sooner he could leave. He'd take a taxi back to the resort to fetch his car, then... that was as far as his thoughts could take him. What then?

The stairs diverged. To the right lay the main reception and the airless waiting room. He took the left flight, rising to a corridor that overlooked the courtyard. The first office at the top of the stairs was spacious and air-conditioned. The middle-aged secretary within barely glanced up from her computer screen as Rik tapped on the door and pushed it all the way open. "How may I help you, Mr...?"

"You can call me Rik."

She looked up at him over the top of her tortoiseshell spectacles and her eyes widened. He had her full attention now. This was the one place in the islands where his face was instantly recognised. She blushed and smoothed back her thick swathe of dark hair. "Oh, I'm so sorry..."

"Is the mayor in?"

"Yes, of course he is." Then she caught sight of Kenzie and her voice faltered. "That is..." She dropped her eyes. Meaning he was in for Rik, but not for anyone else. Now that was the kind of reaction he was more used to getting.

For the first time he wondered how it might feel to be the one forced to wait in the airless waiting room. At least he hadn't yet fallen so far.

"My friend here would like a few minutes with the mayor, if that's at all possible?"

The secretary hesitated, casting another glance past his shoulder to Kenzie. Rik had spent enough time on Los Pajaros to interpret that look. The only women with any authority in these islands – the only women who'd have any business with the mayor – were mature and respected. They weren't pretty young things.

He arched an eyebrow.

"I'll check." The secretary slid out of her chair and hurried to the connecting door, eager to shift the decision of whether to let the foreign girl into the inner sanctum to someone else.

She reappeared scarcely a moment later, smoothing her hair once again. "You may go in."

Rik held the door to the mayor's office open for Kenzie.

"Bravo," she whispered as she brushed past.

He didn't respond. The swift contact between their bodies, the whiff of feminine perfume, her low husky whisper, and the sudden, electrifying heat that flashed between them left him momentarily dazzled. Last night's bender was having some interesting side effects.

The mayor's office was of colonial proportions, dwarfing the massive mahogany desk he sat behind. The purr of the air-con was subtle, but its effect was not.

The mayor's tense smile suggested impatience beneath the politeness as he rose to his full height. "How may I assist you, Your..."

Behind Kenzie's back, Rik furiously shook his head as he cut him off. "Thank you for seeing us, sir. This is Kenzie Cole and she has a request to make of you."

"More of a business proposition." She turned on the same megawatt smile she'd used on him the night before, to pretty much the same effect. The mayor's smile looked a little less forced as he waved them to sit.

Not one to tempt fate, Rik stepped back. When Kenzie turned

to look for him, he shrugged as if to say, *the floor's all yours*, and leaned back against the doorframe, crossing his arms over his chest.

She turned her back on him, focussing all her attention on the mayor, and Rik breathed an internal sigh of relief.

Kenzie was pretty impressive when she turned on the charm. Just flirtatious enough to catch the mayor's interest, just professional enough to be taken seriously. She pulled out a folder from the small rucksack she carried, presenting facts and figures. The mayor leaned closer at the words 'jobs for your laid off ship builders.'

Even Rik stood straighter. Kenzie had done her homework.

Next to tourism, the yacht building business had been Los Pajaros' biggest employer until the recession slashed the demand for such luxuries. Kenzie proposed using the workers who'd lost their jobs to build the pirate ships needed for the film. "It would only be a few months' work, of course, but that's better than nothing, isn't it?"

She sent the mayor another winning smile and he melted. Rik nearly did too. Or he would have, if his entire body hadn't been hard.

The mayor beamed. "You have my full support. I will email the harbour master and ask him to provide you with a boat and an escort. Where do you want to take your photographs?"

Kenzie pulled aerial maps from her folder. "These are the islands I'd like to visit, especially these two – Corona and Tortuga."

Rik stiffened.

The mayor leaned back in his chair and shook his head. "Not possible."

Kenzie's eyes widened in disbelief. "Why not? You just told me I had your full support."

The mayor cast a beseeching look at Rik.

He pushed away from the doorframe. "Corona is private property."

Her brow furrowed. He didn't need to be a mind reader to know she was wondering why Corona was marked on every map as government property if it was private. "And Tortuga?"

Rik and the mayor exchanged a look, and it was Rik who answered again. "Tortuga is a breeding ground for sea turtles."

"It's not a nature sanctuary – I checked. Besides, the hatching season will be well over by the time we shoot."

The mayor's mouth set in a grim line. "No one from these islands has set foot on Isla Tortuga in over three centuries."

The disbelief on Kenzie's face turned to incredulity. "Why ever not?"

The mayor squirmed. "It's haunted."

Rik gave her credit for not laughing.

"I'm not superstitious. If our film crew aren't from these islands and don't mind working there, would you give us permission to film on Tortuga?"

He gave her credit for not giving up either.

Again, the mayor glanced at Rik, this time for approval. The poor man's dilemma was clear. The local economy could do with an injection of capital and a higher international profile. But Tortuga...

Rik nodded.

"I will," the mayor answered Kenzie.

"Thank you. Is there anyone who isn't from these islands who could take me there to photograph the place?"

The mayor paused only a fraction of a second before he looked at Rik. "You have a boat. Could you take her?"

Oh no. That wasn't part of his plan for the rest of the day. Or ever.

Not to mention the mere thought of being on a boat was making him feel green again. He shook his head. "Not today."

"Do you have anything better to do tomorrow, then?"

Of course the mayor knew he had nothing better to do. The mayor knew everything that went on around these islands.

Kenzie also turned to look at him, expectant. But where the mayor's eyes held hope, hers held an entirely different expression. Reluctance.

37

She'd felt the attraction too. And she didn't want to.

Rik shut his eyes, blocking out both their faces.

He knew exactly what tomorrow held. It would be the same as every other day. The sun would shine. He'd wake late, and go for a swim to clear the fuzziness in his head. By the time his arms and legs were too tired to swim any further, he'd wash up on the beach. And that's when the emptiness would hit.

He would spend the rest of his day trying to fill that emptiness. He would run on the beach, or take Adam's boat out, or he'd drink. And he'd already done enough of all these things to last a lifetime.

Even if it was just a boat ride to Tortuga, it beat spending another day in Adam's guesthouse while the walls pressed in on him. But he was done with helping people, unless there was something in it for him. And there was only one thing Kenzie had that he wanted…

Now that was an interesting idea.

He shrugged. "Okay."

Relief crossed the mayor's face. He turned back to Kenzie. "If your director likes the island, then you build your boats on Los Pajaros and you accommodate your crew on Los Pajaros, and you film on Tortuga." *Translation: you spend your money here on Los Pajaros.* "But you must promise me that no islanders will have to go to Tortuga."

"Agreed. Do we have a deal?" Kenzie offered the mayor a courteous handshake.

"Deal." The mayor took Kenzie's hand, but instead of the expected shake, he bowed over their joined hands in the local custom.

Rik held the door open for her, but this time she was careful to avoid contact as she passed. Her scent still slammed into him, though.

He grinned. His body was taking over from his brain. That was an interesting first. He knew passion didn't last and that it burned out far too quickly, but he didn't care. She was only passing through. For just this once, he wanted to be like every other man and indulge his desires.

So she thought she didn't want a man like him, a purposeless drifter with tattoos. And she didn't trust him. Never mind. He could work with that. He'd make her want him, and she wouldn't be able to resist.

Head high.

Chapter Four

@KenzieCole101: Who knew pirates still ruled the Caribbean?

They stood on the pavement beside her rental car. Kenzie shifted, uncomfortably hot inside her own skin. She'd scarcely been able to concentrate throughout the meeting with the scorching awareness of Rik's presence behind her, and the effort was starting to take its toll.

Or perhaps it was just the heat. Or last night's lack of sleep.

It was most certainly not physical attraction making her forget why she was here, or her vow to Lee. And it sure as hell couldn't be the memory of those inked biceps making her want to indulge her fetish for bad boys.

She wasn't that weak, was she, after everything she'd already been through?

"So what now?" She looked at the palm trees lining the esplanade, at the sizzling tar at her feet...anywhere but towards Rik.

"Now I take you home."

At that, her gaze flew to his, horror that he'd read her thoughts tainting her cheeks.

"I need to fetch my car, remember?" That mocking look was back in his eyes.

His car. Of course. She hoped he believed her blush was due

to the midday sun burning down.

She moved to the driver's side but Rik shook his head and held out his hand. "This time I drive."

She hesitated. While there was something in his tone that demanded obedience, it also made her skin crawl. He might not have any right to a title these days but he still acted like he ruled the world. Bloody Golden Boys.

But she had several ex-boyfriends and a 'perfect' big bother who'd helped her develop an immunity to men who believed the world would do their bidding. Just because the rest of the world thought they had it all didn't mean they weren't all douches. In her experience, men like Rik could charm the pants off you in one breath then make you feel like a piece of shit with the next.

And she wasn't going to let anyone make her feel like that again.

She tossed the car keys at him. "Fine."

He didn't take them back the way they'd come. Instead, he drove along the edge of the harbour, out the other side of town and onto a rutted tar road that snaked around the steeply peaked mountain that had once been a volcano.

The road climbed higher and higher up the side of the mountain, twisting and turning, until her knuckles were white with a tension that wasn't entirely induced by the cliff edge a few feet from the car's tyres.

It may have been centuries since the volcano was last active, but she was sure the atmosphere inside the car would register on the Volcanic Explosivity Index. If she thought she'd been aware of him in the mayor's office, it was nothing compared to her awareness of him inside the tight confines of the little car.

He slowed the car, shifting gear, the fabric of his jeans pulling taut across his thighs. She swallowed and looked away. "I thought we were going back to the hotel?"

"We are. I'm taking you back via the scenic route."

He pulled the car into a layby. The vegetation on this side of the mountain was low scrub, allowing unparalleled views. On the wide plain below them were the sugar cane fields that were still the island's most profitable export.

Rik leaned across her, and her whole body went on high alert. Defcon one. Danger of explosion imminent.

Remember him drunk and passed out, you stupid girl. That ought to calm the hormones.

A chain of small islands curved out from Los Pajaros. The charter boat had taken her to the nearest of those. At the furthest tip of the curve a smudge of green was visible on the distant horizon. "That's Tortuga." Rik said, pointing out her window. "Corona isn't visible from here." His voice sounded almost wistful.

She blinked to clear the dancing spots before her eyes and the fog in her brain, relieved when Rik returned both his hands to the steering wheel and re-started the car.

Sleep, that's what she needed. She was an eight hours a night girl and once she'd had an uninterrupted night of sleep, she would stop feeling this raw sexual tension that seemed to be zipping up and down her body. She rubbed her arms.

The road twisted and turned around the dormant volcano, away from the flat plain and the sugar cane fields, gradually descending through a plantation of banana trees to more familiar terrain; dense tropical vegetation, idyllic sandy beaches, and the lush resorts where tourists played in the sunshine.

Rik turned the car in through the gates of her hotel, into the long palm-fringed avenue with golf greens on either side. The resort buildings rose up before them, gleaming white and tiered like a wedding cake.

"So what's the plan for tomorrow?" she asked as he parked her rental beside his.

"I'll meet you in the hotel reception at ten."

She rolled her eyes. "Now where've I heard that before? How can I be sure you'll be there?"

His dark eyes glittered. "I'll be there."

He held out his palm with her car keys. His hand was tanned

and oddly roughened, not as smooth and manicured as she'd expected of a prince. Gingerly, she took the car keys from him, careful not to touch him in case she combusted.

He raised an eyebrow. "*My* keys?"

She flushed, the heat burning her skin. "Of course." She fumbled in her rucksack for his car keys, and held them out less carefully. His fingers stroked the sensitive flesh of her palm as he took them. His gaze fixed on her hand, and he smiled. Then he opened the car door and climbed out.

"Until tomorrow," he said, slamming the door closed.

She nodded, mute. It was a long time before she managed to move. Only when his flashy car roared to deafening life and slid out of its parking bay, did she open her own door. It was as though his touch had short-circuited the wiring in her body.

She had a dreadful suspicion that Lee was going to be very, very disappointed in her when she got back to Blighty.

"Damn him."

***

@KenzieCole101: @LeeHill Is Neil in a huff that I got the permission?

@LeeHill: @KenzieCole101 He's moaning about cost of travelling caterers & labour but the Director's smiling like he just came. Clock's still ticking.

@KenzieCole101: @LeeHill Any word on how the other scouts are doing?

@Lee Hill: @KenzieCole101 The scout on BVI has connections with Richard Branson. You need to hurry with your pics.

Kenzie rubbed her temple. As one of the film's art directors, Lee had not only got her this gig but also had access to all the inside intel, for which Kenzie was grateful. She needed every bit of help she could get. But she was running out of time. Tortuga had better deliver or some other scout would get the glory.

It was ten the next morning and she waited in the hotel's reception, on exactly the same velveteen banquette where Rik had lain the other night. Her foot tapped nervously on the tiled floor as she typed a final response to her flatmate.

She could do this. She was going to return to London a success. She could feel her destiny drawing closer, whatever it was, and Rik wasn't going to distract her from her goal. He wasn't a pirate, he was a prince. She didn't like princes. She wasn't a Disney kind of girl. Well, except for Flynn Rider...

She strained to hear the distinctive roar of the sports car, so when Rik strode into reception, not from the car park but from the gardens, he caught her by surprise. Which was *so* not a good way to start the day. She frowned. "Where's your car?"

"Good morning to you too." He grinned and hefted her camera bag onto his shoulder effortlessly. "We can't get where we're going by car, remember?"

Against her will, she drank him in. Today he wore dark jeans and a white open-necked, collared shirt. The merest hint of tattoo peeked out from beneath his collar. How had he managed to keep that tattoo hidden back in Westerwald? He must have worn nothing but buttoned-up suits and ties. She could hardly imagine it. The Rik who stood before her now looked nothing like a suit and tie kind of man. He looked like a windblown adventurer, with his tan, his days' old stubble and overlong hair brushing his collar.

He looked like a man who could give Flynn Rider a run for his money.

She followed him through the gardens and down to the resort's pier where a number of pleasure cruisers and luxury fishing boats were docked. She had to run to keep up with his long strides.

He definitely appeared in better shape today, which was just as

44

well since he'd be transporting her across open ocean, but did he have to keep wrong-footing her? He was not a man she wanted to let have the upper hand. She wasn't sure her willpower would withstand the test.

At around forty feet, Rik's yacht wasn't the biggest moored alongside the pier, but it was the sleekest, and definitely the most immaculate. Kenzie didn't know much about boats, but it looked impressive; white and very neat, its wooden deck uncluttered by the ropes and accoutrements of its neighbours. It was certainly more elegant than the workhorse motorboat she'd been skippered around in before.

"Can you sail this thing alone?" she asked, eyeing the mast with its furled sail in trepidation.

"*This thing* is a single-handed boat. And she has an engine."

He was laughing at her. She breathed deeply. She was lucky to be going to Tortuga at all. She could put up with anything he threw at her.

He held out his hand to help her on board, but she ignored it, grasped the railing and hoisted herself up onto the deck. Okay, so it wasn't elegant, but it sure beat the heart-fluttering sensation which was sure to accompany his touch.

Rik unsecured the ropes that tethered the boat to the dock, hopped onboard, and made his way nimbly to the helm while Kenzie was still trying to find her balance.

He stowed her camera bag in a locker beneath the wheel. She perched on the cushioned bench beside him and settled her wide-brimmed sun hat on her head and her sunglasses on her face. "How long will it take us to get there?"

"Wind's a good twenty knots, so I'd say a little over an hour. You're welcome to make yourself comfortable in the cabin, if you'd like."

"No thanks. The sun is shining. Where I'm from that's a pretty big deal and not to be missed." Even though she had a tendency to freckle in even the weakest British sun.

45

In spite of the complete inappropriateness of present company, she also didn't want to miss the impressive view up here on deck. Just because she shouldn't touch, didn't mean she couldn't look.... right?

She sneaked more than a few peeks as he rolled up his sleeves, revealing another glimpse of ink and some pretty fine muscle.

He hardly seemed to notice her as he unfurled the sails, edged the boat away from the dock, and set course out to sea. The boat picked up speed as they hit open water and the sails filled.

He was right about the single-handed thing. Everything seemed to be rigged to operate from the helm with a minimum amount of effort. Trimming the sails took just enough labour that she could appreciate why his hands weren't as lily-soft as she'd expected. He wasn't afraid to use them.

She shivered at that thought.

They weren't alone. There were other boats, pleasure craft and fishing boats, plying the smooth, blue sea between the islands, and in the distance she spotted the ferry that ran between the main island of Los Pajaros and the smaller inhabited island of Arelat.

She recognised a few of the islands they passed from her tour with the charter boat. Popular water sport spots jostled alongside tiki bars and restaurants that served fish pulled straight from the sea. If she got this right, the film crew were going to be in heaven on their days off.

The islands grew further apart and less populated. The last of the islands she'd toured previously was Sandy Bar, literally nothing more than a massive dune spotted with palm trees.

Then they were into virgin territory.

"So where are you from?" Rik asked, settling back beside her in the cockpit.

"England."

"No kidding. I meant where in England are you from?"

"Hertfordshire born and bred, in a place you've probably never heard of. St Albans."

"Roman ruins, a duck pond and The Waffle House, right?"

Wow. How on earth did a prince of a European nation know The Waffle House? But since she wasn't supposed to know who he was, she asked only "you've been there?"

"I have a friend who lives nearby. Have you ever been on a yacht before?"

As it happens, she had. It wasn't exactly a memory she was proud of, though. Bad Boy Number One had been a promising footballer. He'd hung with a crowd who she'd thought had it all – money, beauty, dazzlingly bright futures, while she'd been an ordinary girl from an ordinary end of terrace house in suburbia with nothing more than big dreams.

They'd taken her sailing around Cowes once and all got horribly drunk – except Kenzie who'd done her usual and tried to be responsible and fix things. But as the sea had grown rougher and the rain lashed down on them, and her footballer was too busy being sick over the railings, she hadn't been able to fix anything. By the time the Coastguard rescued them she'd been in full-scale panic mode, convinced they were all going to drown.

They'd got off with nothing more than a slap on the wrist – her first experience of the kind of influence money could buy – but they'd made the papers and her parents had been livid.

It wasn't the only time she'd made the tabloids. After a while, her parents had stopped being livid. They'd just been disappointed. Still were, even though those days were long gone.

She cringed now. That was all going to change. They'd see, the whole world would see, that she wasn't just a screw up. That she really was destined for great things.

She'd felt it since she was a child, this feeling that there was something *more* for her out there. A couple of times she'd thought she'd found it, like with Bad Boy Number Two, Charlie, heir to an Earldom. Another of those Golden Boys who seemed to have it all. But again, it had been nothing but the brass ring.

Still, she wasn't going to give up the faith. Things always worked out in the end. If she didn't believe that, she'd have been a basket case long before now.

"I have," she answered Rik.

"Great. You take the wheel. I'm going down to get us a drink. Just keep her straight."

Oh no! She wasn't going to relive that particular memory!

But before she could protest, Rik abandoned her at the helm and disappeared through the hatch into the cabin. She clung to the wheel for dear life and concentrated on keeping the boat headed straight.

Please, please don't let Rik get drunk again. What would she do on her own on a boat in the middle of the ocean? What if there were rocks or reefs or...?

This wasn't the Isle of Wight and she had no idea who to call for help. Would any local even come to her aid if they were too scared to set foot on Tortuga? They'd probably leave her to the sharks.

Her hands gripped the wheel so tight her knuckles turned white.

She forced herself to breathe as she anxiously scanned the sky. Clear and blue and wide, with only the fluffiest of clouds to be seen.

Was the beam supposed to move like that?

She gripped the wheel harder. On the day at Cowes, the weather had also started like this. But it hadn't taken long for the wind to pick up and the sea to turn into a raging monster.

When Rik finally re-emerged, juggling two bottles of water and two cans of pop – and not a beer in sight – she nearly threw herself at him in relief.

"I wasn't sure what you wanted?" he asked, holding out the selection.

She prised her grip from the wheel and smacked his chest.

"Ow, what was that for?"

"Don't do that to me again!"

"Do what?" his brow furrowed.

"Abandon me like that." She took a bottle of water from him and sagged back on the bench, opened it and glugged down the refreshing liquid.

That was bad boys all over. Thought of no-one but themselves, dumped you when it suited them, and left you to carry the can. She was so over it.

***

@KenzieCole101: I'm so excited I could throw up. Oh wait, maybe that's just seasickness.

Rik adjusted the course of the boat and took a swig from his water bottle. She'd been scared, and he couldn't work out why. The sea was calm as a lake today, the wind just right, visibility good. And out here, a few miles off Isla Tortuga, there was little chance of other traffic.

Kenzie was certainly nothing like the women he'd dated before. She appeared confident and capable, yet she clearly wasn't as self-assured as she seemed. Teresa would never have gone to pieces like that. Nor would his ex-girlfriend have looked at him with that mix of relief, anger and heat.

Their relationship had been uncomplicated and easy, and he'd never tried to make it anything more. He'd never wondered what Teresa was thinking. With the clarity of hindsight he had to admit he'd never really cared enough to find out.

"We'll need to sail around to the leeward side of the island to the break in the reef," he said, altering their course a little. "There's a deep lagoon that side that might work for your pirate ship."

Kenzie lifted her head, instantly intrigued. "You've been here before?"

"A few times. My brother and I..." he swallowed. "We used to spend part of our summer holidays here in the islands. When we were teens we dared each other to sail to Tortuga. Teenage boys don't believe in curses..." He pressed his lips together.

They'd come not once, but dozens of times over the years,

feeling brave and invulnerable. He was starting to believe in the curse now, though. He'd lost everything he ever loved, and Max had been forced to give up on his dreams, his passion for wine making. If that wasn't a curse, he didn't know what was.

Although, Max must have found a new passion to replace the old if he was getting married. Rik hadn't paid much thought to the bride before now, but fleetingly he wondered what kind of woman had managed to get his footloose younger brother to the altar.

Either that, or he'd realised the benefit of a partner to share the burden. Though why he'd chosen some obscure American over a candidate as suitable as Teresa, was anyone's guess.

"You're lucky." Kenzie shielded her eyes as she looked to where Tortuga loomed out of the sea. "My brother and I rarely did stuff together. Our ideas of fun were always so different." She worried her lip again. The stirring in his lower half whenever she did that was starting to feel almost familiar.

He shifted position. "How many siblings do you have?"

"One is more than enough."

"You don't get along?"

She shrugged. "James is okay, but we have nothing in common. He's just so...unadventurous."

"And you are?" He cocked an eyebrow at her, and she blushed and looked away. She certainly looked like an adventurer, in her cargo pants, hiking boots and khaki hat, but the image that flashed through his mind at her blush had absolutely nothing to do with clothing. No clothing at all, in fact.

"Why do the locals believe the island is haunted?" she asked, keeping her gaze averted.

"Not so much haunted as cursed. It's said that anyone who visits Tortuga will suffer lifelong grief and heartache." And violent death.

"Why?"

"There's a local legend that a sorcerer cast a curse on the island after he lost the love of his life to another man, a pirate from Tortuga."

Rik completely understood that urge for revenge. Those first weeks after he'd arrived in Los Pajaros he'd been angry at the world, and his loss had been far greater than the loss of a prospective wife. After all, wasn't the love for one's nation far greater than love for a woman?

He breathed out heavily. It was just a tragedy that had happened a long time ago. He hadn't reached this point in his life because of some old curse. He was here because his life had been built on lies, and his mother, one of only three people in the world he'd trusted implicitly, had been the liar.

He concentrated on looking for the break in the coral reef that circled the island, sheltering Tortuga's bays from the open sea. He'd swum and snorkelled in these coves often enough to know where the deepest channels were, where the tide pulled hardest, where the fish were most plentiful. And also where the wrecks were.

"You'll need to mark this entrance into the lagoon with buoys. And since it's illegal to drop anchor on the reef itself to protect the corals, I'd recommend keeping bigger boats out beyond the reef and using smaller boats to get in close. You could build a mooring for them in one of the coves close to the lagoon."

Kenzie pulled a notebook and pen from a side pocket of her rucksack and began scribbling notes.

Rik circled the island to a cove that was deep enough to get them in close to the shore. Kenzie sat up straighter, her gaze fixed on the sandy beach.

He dropped the anchor and furled the sails. "I'll show you a bay later that I'd recommend for a pier. Since the locals won't come here, you'll need to bring your own labour and your own boat crews."

She nodded. "There'll be a lot of extra costs, but my producer wasn't too fazed when I spoke to him last night. The tax benefits the mayor agreed to probably helped." She grinned. "And he was probably so stunned I'd actually got permission for us to film here. Neil never expected me to get this far."

51

"What is it with you and your boss?"

She shrugged, looking away. "Like everyone else, he underestimated me. Let's get going, shall we?"

He dropped the dinghy over the side, climbed down the swimming ladder, then turned to help Kenzie, allowing his hands to linger on her waist as he lifted her down. The buzz between them was as delicious as he remembered.

She flicked a glance up at him, her big blue eyes wide and startled beneath the long, pale eyelashes. "You can let me go now."

"What if I don't want to?" he teased, enjoying her blush. Kenzie Cole made him want to do bad, bad things. He was going to enjoy exacting his payment from her.

He withdrew his hands and bent down to fire up the outboard motor. There was no need to hurry this. Seduction was better taken slowly. And by the time he got what he wanted from her, Kenzie would be begging for him to take it.

But for a moment, a sense of disquiet unnerved him. The images he'd pictured in that brief moment of contact were not the sort of things he'd contemplated doing with any other woman before. Kenzie definitely had something he wanted. And with each passing day he seemed to want it more. With the kind of passion he didn't trust and didn't want.

When the dinghy slid up onto the hot white sand, she jumped out as if she couldn't get away fast enough. But she wasn't looking at him. The blush was gone, but her face was still flushed, her eyes alight now with excitement. A purely professional excitement.

By the time he'd pulled the dinghy above the high tide line, she'd already started snapping photographs, a panoramic view of the bay.

Then she began jotting notes in her book. "What's the name of this bay?" she called over her shoulder.

"It doesn't have a name. We're modern day explorers. You can call it whatever you like."

She grinned. "I think I'll call it the Bay of Hope, then."

"Esperanza," he suggested, resisting the urge to roll his eyes.

He'd been to Tortuga several times over the last few months and hope was the one thing he hadn't found here.

Once she'd taken her pictures and made her notes, they picked their way through the scrubby brush to reach the neighbouring bay.

A couple of hours later and Rik was starting to feel the effects of the midday heat. He sat on the sand in the shade of a Royal Poinciana tree and pulled water bottles and sandwich packets out of his rucksack.

"You need a break," he called to Kenzie.

He had to admire her tenacity. She was not as fragile as she appeared. She'd kept up a rigorous pace as they hiked from bay to bay and still looked fresh as a flower, if a little flushed. Her hair clung damply to her neck and forehead, curling slightly in the heat. She flopped down beside him, gratefully accepted the bottle of water, and began to fan herself with her hat.

"You're getting pink," he observed.

"I know. It's such a pain being this fair. I'm going to be horribly freckled when I get back to England."

"It's cute."

She wrinkled her nose. "*Cute* is not the look I was going for." She looked down the beach and sighed, a deep-throated purr of pleasure. "A couple of days ago I didn't much like the Caribbean. I think I'm changing my mind. Everything seems more here. More colourful, more tasty, more aromatic."

"More arousing." He flashed a quick sidelong glance at her and grinned.

Although he hadn't found these islands particularly arousing before Kenzie had walked into that beach bar.

She stretched out on the sand beside him, rolling onto her back to look up into the tangerine-coloured canopy above. "I think the sorcerer's curse was really a blessing. I'm sure there aren't many unspoilt places like this left in the world. I almost don't want to bring the film crew here."

"But you will."

"I have to. It's my job."

"There are other places, other islands."

"Yes, but there's something special about these islands. Perhaps it's that virgin territory thing. There's never been a big film shoot here before, so I'll be the first to discover it. I can put this place on the map."

"What if it doesn't want to be on any map?"

"Ask the mayor if he agrees with that. Films don't just bring business in the short-term. They bring exposure, which brings tourists. And more tourists means more money and more jobs."

"So is that why you chose to become a location scout. Out of philanthropy?"

She laughed. "No, and if you ask my parents they'll tell you it was a very selfish choice. I became a location scout because it's never boring. Every day is different. Every film shoot is different. I've scouted grand houses and farm cottages, cities and open countryside. And I've met all sorts of interesting people. Like you." Her eyes lit up with a cheeky amusement as she looked at him. "And it's a challenge. It's a whole lot more than just taking pictures. You have to understand what the director wants, the angles and lenses he wants to use. And you need to know the production logistics too, and be a people person." She rolled up onto her elbow to look at him. "Besides, I think if I had to work in an office, doing the same thing every day, I'd go insane."

He used to work in an office, and he missed it. From the day he'd returned home from university, his father had given him his own office in the palace at Neustadt, and he'd assumed many of the duties and responsibilities that had been his father's. He'd never once thought of what he might be missing beyond the palace walls. And he'd never wanted to be anywhere else.

He'd devoted himself to his country and his people, and what had he got in return? Exile.

All because of a routine DNA test.

In spite of everything, he still didn't want to be anywhere else. He'd rather be there in his high-ceilinged office in the palace than here in paradise.

But there was no going back now. Not even for Max's engagement party.

Kenzie tossed the empty sandwich packets and water bottles into the rucksack and jumped up. "Let's get going. We've barely covered half the island. At this rate we'll have to come back tomorrow."

At this rate he was going to need something to keep up with her... and it certainly wasn't those little blue pills. He pushed himself to his feet, in no hurry to get moving.

No, there was no going back. But for the first time in months, he wanted to move forward. He looked forward to tomorrow.

Chapter Five

@KenzieCole101: I scaled mountains today – and have the pictures to prove it!

@LeeHill: @KenzieCole101 Knew you could do it! Crack open that minibar to celebrate.

@LeeHill: @KenzieCole101 PS: Simba sends his love. He misses you.

@KenzieCole101: @LeeHill Scratch him behind his ears for me

Kenzie arrived back in Los Pajaros more tired, more dusty and more freckled than she'd felt any other day she'd been here. They'd barely managed to explore half the bays and beaches of Tortuga before the sun began to dip and they'd headed home. But she had enough to make the director salivate, she was sure of that.

Tomorrow Rik would take her back so they could scout the island's forested interior for the remaining locations on her list.

It had been a good day. No, it had been a great day.

She didn't need a drink tonight with the same desperation as the night she'd met Rik, but she wanted to celebrate and once again the minibar in her room wasn't going to cut it.

So as Rik handed her across the gap between boat and dock, she glanced up at him, feeling oddly shy. "Would you like a drink before you go?"

His answering grin definitely wasn't shy. It was downright cocky, reminding her for a sickening moment of Charlie's lopsided smile, and for half a second she regretted asking. "I've got a better idea. Join me for dinner."

It wasn't a question, she noticed. But her hackles no longer took the bait. Perhaps having spent a day in his presence she'd become immune to that commanding tone.

However, she definitely hadn't grown immune to what he did to all the other parts of her body. Rik may have played the gentleman rather than the bad boy all day, but his tiny, fleeting touches were driving her insane. A hand on her elbow to help her over a log, a brush of her brow to wipe away a smudge... though she was pretty sure he'd made that last one up.

It was those less immune parts that started an excited jig at the thought of not having to call it quits on this day just yet.

But dinner? That was a far bigger commitment than a drink at the beach bar. And dinner with a devastating bad boy could lead to very bad places, as she knew from bitter experience. Still, she wasn't that girl any more. She could handle a civilised, platonic meal out without losing all self-respect.

"We have an early start tomorrow," she said, clinging to common sense but knowing it was a battle she was about to lose.

"You'll still get your precious eight hours," he teased.

And there it came, her impulsive heart over-ruling her oh-so-sensible brain. "Okay, I'd love dinner. The resort has a really good haute cuisine restaurant."

"No, not the resort. There's a seafood place in town I think you'll enjoy."

No, no, no, no. She was rapidly losing control here. She grabbed at the last lifeline she could find. "But you didn't bring a car."

"We'll go by boat." Then incorrectly interpreting the quick flash

57

of panic across her face: "That first night was a one off. I won't get drunk again and I'll get you back here in one piece."

It wasn't his sailing ability she didn't trust. She'd had plenty of opportunity today to watch him work. He might not talk much, but he seemed very competent. What she didn't trust were her own instincts and her own ability to resist temptation. Three times she'd already got it very, very wrong, and no-one ever said 'Fourth time's the charm.'

And in the dark, with the moonlight and the roll of the ocean...

She sent up a swift prayer to the gods to protect what was left of her heart, and nodded. "I'll need to upload my photos and send them to London before we leave, though." And she needed a shower. And she wondered if the resort boutique would still be open. "I'll meet you back here in an hour?"

She hoped she hadn't just made a terrible mistake agreeing to dinner.

She got back to the boat an hour and a half later, flustered, out of breath, her hair already escaping from its ponytail.

"I'm so sorry," she said, instinctively taking the hand Rik held out to her and instantly regretting it. "Neil called to talk through what I'd sent him and I couldn't get rid of him."

Not that she'd wanted to. It was really nice to hear the words "well done, good job". It had put her on such a high she hadn't bothered to return her mother's call. The inevitable disappointment in *that* conversation would definitely have killed her buzz.

Rik still had hold of her hand. "Look at that – you're a girl!" His voice sounded indifferent, but his eyes were anything but.

She pretended a frown. "Of course I'm a girl."

"I thought you didn't own a dress?"

She waved a hand, dismissing the question and hoping her blush didn't give her away. "I found this old thing in the bottom of the suitcase," she lied.

The hotel's boutique had still been open, and this short cocktail dress in a soft, clingy midnight blue had been an easy choice.

It reminded her of Rik's eyes, so dark a shade of blue they were almost black. The dress was too posh to go with the espadrilles but she didn't want to look like she'd made too much effort.

Though the fact she was wearing make-up for the first time in months would have tipped off anyone who knew her.

Rik settled himself behind the wheel, and she took her now familiar spot on the cushioned bench beside him. The dress rode up her thighs, and she had to sit uncomfortably upright to keep her modesty. Perhaps she should have stuck with cargo pants after all.

This time Rik kept the sails furled and used the engine. They headed out to sea, but instead of turning left towards Fredrikshafen, he turned the boat right.

"Isn't town the other way?" she asked.

"If you're a tourist. The locals prefer the smaller fishing town of Christianstad on the other side of the island. The restaurants there aren't priced for the day visitors from the cruise ships." He grinned. "Are you up for a little adventure?"

"Always." Though now she really wished she'd stuck with cargo pants and a tee shirt.

The boat hugged the shoreline and she was able to appreciate the wild beauty of the island in the evening light. She'd been so focussed on finding the locations listed on the detailed location brief she'd been given that she'd nearly missed the magic which was right under her nose.

On the horizon, the sun was a ball of fire, staining the sea crimson. As it sank, both sea and sky faded to vivid pinks and oranges, growing darker and darker until the light was gone, leaving nothing but a flash of green light so fast she wondered if she'd imagined it. Then the velvet darkness wrapped around them.

No lingering sunsets here in the tropics. It was all or nothing.

"Wow, that was incredible." She breathed out, her voice barely above a whisper, afraid she might break the magic spell.

"The sunsets are more spectacular in the winter months. There's too much haze in the air in summer." Rik turned the boat into an inlet between two high outcrops of land, mere shadows against the night sky.

In the apex of the bay, pinpricks of light bloomed out of the darkness as they drew nearer, turning into a jumble of single-storey houses. This was definitely not Fredrikshafen, with its massive modern marina, stylish boutiques and bright lights. The pier where Rik moored his boat consisted of rickety planks, lit only by swaying lanterns, and theirs was the only yacht amongst the fishing skiffs and dories.

"I guarantee this is the best meal you'll eat in all the islands." He took her hand as they walked down the pier.

She hoped so. She was starving. Those sandwiches they'd shared on the beach at Tortuga seemed light years away.

The restaurant was little more than a thatched bar, open to the elements on all sides, with mismatched tables and chairs set out on a wooden deck overhanging the sea. A few locals in work-roughened clothes sat at the bar, and the only occupants of the deck were a handful of young men in gaudy shirts and board shorts drinking beers.

"Instructors from the local scuba school," Rik said, following her gaze.

The instructors waved and the locals at the bar greeted him in a language she didn't recognise. Kenzie wondered if they knew who he really was – or at least who he had been. Their looks held respect, but none of the awe the mayor seemed to hold him in.

Rik let go of her hand to return their greetings, and she instantly felt the loss of the contact. Then he placed his hand on her lower back to direct her onto the deck. Familiar, slow heat radiated out from his touch.

The kind of heat that made that oh-so-sensible brain of hers reel.

She hadn't known until now how much she missed human contact. Cuddling Lee's cat was all well and fine but it didn't come close to the heart-thumping touch of a gorgeous man.

Rik chose a table right on the very edge of the deck, away from the others, where a light breeze rolled in off the sea, smelling of adventure and anticipation.

A beaming waiter appeared at their side. "Welcome back, Mr Rik."

"Hello Juan."

Juan lit the candles on the table, covering them with sawn-off plastic bottles to keep the lively breeze from extinguishing them.

There were no menus, just a chalkboard listing the day's catch. The array of cocktails however, painted in bright-coloured lettering on a board over the bar, was impressive.

"What would you like?" Rik asked.

"A mojito." It was her favourite cocktail, but here, beneath the star-spangled velvet sky, seemed a far better place to enjoy one than in a densely packed London club. She sighed and stretched back in her seat, allowing contentment and the lazy tropical heat to seep into her limbs.

"Make that two."

When Juan left, she couldn't resist teasing: "No rum and cola tonight?"

Rik pulled a face. "I'll be happy never to taste it again. I made a fool of myself the other night, and I apologise. I offer you my thanks for assisting me."

Now he sounded like a prince. She shrugged. "It's what anyone would have done."

"No, not anyone."

"Yeah, you're right. I'm just a sucker for trouble." That's what following one's instincts tended to do for a girl. She glanced back at the bar. "So what was the special occasion you were celebrating the other night?"

He was silent for so long she was almost sure he wasn't going to answer.

"It was my birthday."

And he'd been alone.

Her heart squeezed tight, and the evening air filled with the sounds of voices from the bar and the breakers crashing on rocks below their deck.

"I'm sorry," she managed at last. She looked quickly away again. "This isn't the sort of place I'd have thought you'd visit." She bit her lip. She wasn't supposed to know who he was. Wasn't supposed to care either.

"Oh? What sort of place do you think I belong?" he asked. The mocking tone was back.

"You drive a Lamborghini and own a yacht. I'd have thought you'd be five star luxury all the way."

"I hope I haven't disappointed you?" He was definitely mocking her.

"Not at all. I'm done with trust fund babies. My best friend Lee and I have sworn that from now on we're only dating men who have real jobs and earn their money the old-fashioned way."

Rik grinned. "Sounds dull. I'd have expected something more adventurous from you. Besides, some would say inheriting it *is* the old-fashioned way."

She scowled. "You know what I mean."

"Then you'll be pleased to know that neither the Lamborghini nor the yacht are mine. They belong to a friend who's kindly letting me stay in his guesthouse."

"Very pleased." She gave up trying to secure the paper napkin in her lap and instead wedged it under the cutlery.

Still didn't mean she was going to let the setting or the man get to her head. Just because he didn't own the bling didn't mean he was a regular Joe with a job. She'd bet her beloved camera that, deposed or not, the former prince had a trust fund. He certainly had all the arrogance that went with it, though he didn't look particularly arrogant right now. Sobriety suited Rik. He seemed a whole lot happier today. No, maybe not happy. There was a constant brooding darkness in his eyes, and he never truly relaxed, but at least he was smiling more today.

Juan delivered their mojitos along with a platter of pieces of pale white meat on a bed of lettuce.

"What's this?" she asked.

"It's raw conch marinated in lime juice, a local delicacy."

"Aren't conches shells?"

"Shellfish. You're not allergic?"

She shook her head. "I can eat anything. Once." She took a fortifying sip of her mojito first. Yum. Definitely better than any she'd had before. Then she stuck her fork into a piece of conch, closed her eyes and tasted.

An explosion of flavour hit her tongue. The conch was chewy, a little like calamari, but full of subtle flavours. "Wow! It's almost better than sex."

He grinned. "Then you obviously haven't been having the right kind of sex."

"I said almost."

"You're not sorry I brought you here?"

No. Not sorry he'd brought her to this restaurant and not sorry she'd agreed to dinner. This was way better than room service alone in a bland hotel room. And the mojito was way better than those over-priced little bottles of wine in the minibar.

Rik sipped his drink, his expression becoming pained. "This reminds me of something..." He swallowed. "Oh god! It tastes like your concierge's hangover remedy." He pushed the glass towards her. "Another drink I may never be able to face again."

Someone fired up a barbecue, and the sizzling aroma of grilling fish filled the air. Kenzie's stomach started doing flick-flacks.

Rik lazed back in his chair. "So tell me about this man who's put you off trust funds."

"It's not just one man. Actually it's probably not any men at all. It's me. I have a tendency to go out with guys who are completely self-absorbed."

Brett, aka Bad Boy Number Three hadn't been a trust fund baby. But he hadn't been a steady job kind of guy either. He'd been a musician, very talented but useless when it came to things like showing up on time or paying bills. She'd ended up supporting him. And bailing him out.

"I'm tired of always being the responsible one and getting nothing in return. From now on I'm going to be selfish. If there's nothing in it for me, then I'm not interested."

She didn't know why she was spilling her guts to Rik. He surely couldn't be interested. Perhaps she was just trying to remind herself.

He smiled and raised his water glass to her. "I'll toast to that. Here's to being selfish and looking out for number one."

Like that was a surprise. Same as every other man she'd been attracted to, he'd probably spent his whole life looking out for himself.

The calypso music in the background cranked up, and the deck began to fill around them, a rowdy Friday night mix of locals and tourists. Not the well-heeled tourists one saw in Fredrikshafen, but the backpacker kind. The sort of people who came to dive and hike, with natural tans rather than the type that came from a spray can.

Her kind of people. She relaxed a little more.

"So what do you do, when you're not ferrying damsels in distress around the islands?" she asked.

His expression shut down. "What's your next assignment?"

Back to playing Mystery Man again. She rolled her eyes. "I have no idea. I fly back to London on Monday evening, and then... who knows?"

"How do you plan ahead?"

"I don't."

He frowned. "So what's your career plan then?"

"There's no point in making plans, since they never work out. I prefer to live in the moment." She might have said the earth was flat, the way he looked at her. She hadn't figured him for a Type A personality.

He raised an eyebrow. "How's that working out for you?"

She laughed and looked around. "I'm here, aren't I? I'm in

paradise and I'm getting paid to be here. What could be better?"

"Everyone should have a five year plan. It's the only way to get ahead."

"So what's your five year plan?"

For a long moment he didn't answer. Then he sighed and rubbed his face. "I'm figuring that out. The plan I had...it didn't work out." The confession seemed to be wrung from him, and she almost felt sorry for him. Almost. But she wasn't falling for the poor little rich boy act again.

"Exactly. A lot of plans don't pan out. But there are always other options. What did you want to be when you were a kid?"

"There's only one thing I ever wanted to be: what I was. I wanted to work in the family business and I did until...I guess you could call it a hostile take-over."

"You never wanted to stretch your wings and try something new?" She couldn't imagine it. Being raised your whole life to do one thing and actually wanting to do it? The earth *would* be flat before she did what everyone else wanted her to do.

Her parents had tried. They still told her she was being selfish for not moving back home to work in the family bakery. They'd also tried to set her up with their accountant more times than she could count.

She couldn't think of anything worse. Spending the rest of her life in suburbia, tied to her parents, the business, an accountant... having to work under her can-do-no-wrong big brother...

She gulped down a mouthful of mojito. It hurt that her own family still knew her so little they thought she'd be happy living that life.

Great, now she felt depressed. Another subject change was needed.

"Have you considered taking up piracy?" she suggested.

Rik frowned, not getting it, and she couldn't blame him. He probably hadn't looked in a mirror lately.

She tried again. "It's not a five year plan exactly, but I heard a rumour that this production company has a film lined up with JJ Abrams. If Neil puts in a good word for me, maybe I can get a job on that one."

"Who is JJ Abrams?"

Her eyes widened. "What rock have you been living under? *Mission Impossible III* … *Star Trek*… The new *Star Wars*? He's just about the biggest director in Hollywood right now."

"I don't really watch films."

"No kidding. What do you do for fun then? Or does drinking in beach bars just about cover it?"

He grinned, and the cloud that seemed to have descended over him lifted a little. "Just about. That's something else I'm working out: how to have fun." His eyes glinted. "You could help me with that."

There was no misunderstanding that glint in his eye. A cold shiver slid down her back. It felt remarkably like anticipation. Or the thrill of the chase, with her as the naive buck in the leopard's sights.

She broke eye contact and looked away, wishing she could use her icy mojito glass to cool her cheeks. Except that would give away just how much he was getting to her. And she suspected he might take that as an invitation.

Juan brought two big earthenware platters to their table, filled with huge grilled lobsters, shelled and fresh from the barbecue, served on a bed of rice.

Kenzie licked her lips. "And what are these?" she asked, pointing at her plate.

"Plantain chips. They're like bananas – sweet." Rik lifted one off his plate and held it to her lips.

Her gaze held his for a fraction of a second before she opened her mouth and took a bite.

"Are you flirting with me?" she asked, once she'd swallowed it down. He was right, it was sweet. Better than plain old potato chips back home.

"Of course. Isn't that what one does when on a date with a beautiful woman?"

She choked on the plantain chip. "This isn't a date!"

"It isn't?" His eyes held that dangerous glitter again. "Dinner, moonlight, pretty woman...sure looks like a date to me."

"Yeah, but I'm leaving in three days."

He grinned. "What difference does that make? It's just a date, not a lifelong commitment." The way his face pulled at that thought, she could guess what he thought of lifelong commitments.

"I don't do one-night stands," she said, as haughtily as she could muster.

No, she had a tendency to throw herself into long, complicated relationships and lose her heart and a piece of herself in the process. And pick up a reputation.

She concentrated on her lobster and pretended that the idea of getting down and dirty with Rik wasn't giving her hot flushes.

He leaned back in his seat and eyed her. "I've never had a one-night stand either, but there's always a first time for everything."

A man who'd never had a one-night stand? Yeah right, and pull the other leg.

Her mojito glass was empty. She chased down the last of the lobster with Rik's untouched drink.

Perhaps it would be different if she just indulged her body for a change, and kept her heart out of it. Perhaps a one-night stand was exactly what she needed.

Three days...that wasn't enough time to lose her heart. Right?

The hot flush headed south. She pressed her thighs together, but that only made it worse.

No, she couldn't. She'd sworn a vow. And that mischief in Rik's eyes definitely put him in the 'off limits, avoid-at-all-costs' category.

"I think you should take me home," she said. Her voice was hoarse. She cleared her throat.

"That was easier than I expected."

She choked again. "I mean...I need to work tomorrow..."

He grinned and rose. "I know what you meant."

Rik dropped cash on the table, then moved to hold her seat for her to stand. Such old-fashioned manners did nothing to ease her erratic pulse. Why couldn't he be a straight-forward jerk and make it easy on her?

Juan waved them out the restaurant with another beaming smile, and then they were back on the boat which suddenly seemed even more intimate than their table at the restaurant had been.

While Rik guided the boat out of the harbour, Kenzie lounged back on the bench, no longer caring that her dress rode up and flashed way too much thigh. She was rewarded by his lingering gaze on her legs.

Good. She hoped his pulse was just as affected as hers. She hoped she drove him just as crazy as he drove her.

The coastline of Los Pajaros shimmered with magic in the dark, tiny fairy lights glittering between the trees, the beaches edged with dancing phosphorescence.

But the real magic show was above. She leaned back on her elbows and looked up. She'd lived close enough to London all her life that the sight of the Milky Way was still a treat. That was one of the best perks of her job – it took her to places where she could escape the light and noise pollution and actually see the stars.

This night sky was a hundred times better than any she'd seen, and she'd travelled enough to have seen a lot of impressive nights.

A balmy breeze stroked over her bare limbs. Her skin felt more alive, almost electric.

Los Pajaros had awakened her senses. Every colour seemed brighter, every experience deeper. The lazy heat that caressed her skin, the rich scents, the tastes...sweet and tart melting together.

And she definitely felt hungry for more. Of everything.

It was as if she'd been only half alive before, and here she was awakened, a new person, a better person.

This sense of possibility was familiar, it was that feeling she'd had as a child, that sense that she could have anything, do anything, be anything. She closed her eyes and breathed it in. She wasn't a screw up. She was a young woman with the world at her feet, and a future, not just a past.

Today could be the beginning of a whole new life.

She sighed, contentment infusing her. Right here in this moment, this was who she was meant to be. And who she was meant to be didn't feel civilised at all. She wanted to throw caution to the wind and live in the moment. She wanted to be wild.

Her stomach knotted in delicious anticipation. She wanted to be wild with Rik.

She and Lee had vowed not to get involved with any man who might be dangerous to their sanity or their heart. But a quick island fling wouldn't constitute *involved*, would it? It wasn't as though she'd see him again after she flew home.

The resort pier emerged out of the darkness too soon. Rik slid the boat in beside the pier and helped her down from the deck. They stood on the shadowy marina, close enough that the heat throbbed between them.

"Thank you for today," she said, still entranced by that heat and unable to step away.

His gaze held hers, sending shivers of anticipation through her. He bent his head, and her breath froze. He was going to kiss her. Yes!

She closed her eyes and tilted her face.

But when his touch came, it wasn't the expected brush of lips across hers. He kissed her cheek. "Good night, Kenzie."

Thank heavens for the dark. He couldn't see her blush, her embarrassment, her disappointment. Damn those mojitos, but she'd wanted him to kiss her.

And he hadn't.

Back to being the girl who just couldn't catch a break when it came to men.

"Good night." She forced as much fake cheer into her voice as she could muster. "Same time, same place tomorrow?"

He nodded and climbed back on the boat, effectively turning his back on her and dismissing her. For a few hours she'd forgotten who he was. What he was.

Clearly they didn't teach manners at Prince Academy. Or how to take advantage of willing damsels in distress. Because right now she was definitely in distress. The kind that even a cold shower wasn't going to fix.

She made her way back along the well-lit path towards the main hotel building. Once her heartbeat returned to normal, or as normal as it had been since Rik slid out of the shadows in the beach bar into full, glorious view, she sighed.

Who the hell was Rik anyway? One minute he was a courteous gentleman, the next a brooding bad boy, then a haughty prince. And don't forget the Type A control freak who thought everyone should have a plan for their lives. Like that had worked for him.

Was Rik a man who would break her heart? Or was he the solid, dependable type?

It didn't matter. This could go nowhere.

But still she wanted him to kiss her. Actually, a whole lot more than kiss her.

She was so screwed. And she certainly wanted to be.

Chapter Six

@KenzieCole101: A new day and a fresh start. God knows I need one of those.

"Did you sleep well?" Rik held out his hand to help her up on deck.

"Like a baby." If she could have crossed her fingers behind her back without him seeing, she would have. It wasn't exactly a lie though. Babies were famous for waking up throughout the night, weren't they?

Mind you, babies probably didn't do their tossing and turning as they wondered if they'd just imagined the undercurrents or whether Rik was toying with her. Or whether his plan was to make her beg for it. Right now, she was a heartbeat away from begging.

She gathered her dignity and headed for the cabin. "I have work to do today."

It was cooler beneath the deck. Though it was barely mid-morning it might as well be midday, the air was so sultry.

She sat at a desk so neat and tidy that it had clearly been arranged by someone with an obsessive compulsive disorder, and pulled her iPad from her rucksack. It would be easier to forget last night's abysmal anti-climax if she kept busy and away from Rik. It would also be easier to keep her rampaging libido under control if she didn't have to actually look at him.

Besides, today she was starting afresh. No more throwing herself at dark, brooding men. No more humiliation. She had a job to do, and she was going to do it, without getting side-tracked.

If another scout pipped her to the post, she'd be nothing more than another name scrolling in the film credits, one among hundreds of other names. Only the glory that went with success-fully pulling off a near impossible feat would be enough to take her from the minor leagues to the majors and establish her as something more than the rich man's arm candy she'd been nearly a decade ago.

"Hey – you have wireless on board!"

She didn't get an answer so she clicked open her inbox.

After half an hour of wondering what Rik was doing, she'd accomplished nothing more than a few tweets. So much for not getting sidetracked.

She powered down the iPad and emerged from the cabin with bottles of water from the fridge. "I brought you something to-"

Rik had removed his shirt. He wore nothing but jeans, and that glistening torso...

The last time she'd seen him shirtless she hadn't fully appreci-ated the beauty of his tattoo. The artistry was phenomenal.

Her mouth watered.

"It's the dragon of Westerwald." Then she bit her tongue. Obviously he knew what it was.

"I was raised there." He hunched his shoulders, almost as though he wanted to shrug the tattoo away. "The wind's up today. We're nearly there."

She cleared her throat and handed him a bottle of water. "I've got great news. The director loves the pictures I sent last night and he wants today's pictures as a matter of urgency. If he likes these too, he and the producer will fly out tomorrow to take a look for themselves."

She was so close to success she could smell it.

"They'll need a boat and a skipper," he said, pouring some of the bottled water over his head and neck. It was like a David Gandy advert coming to breathtaking life right before her eyes.

She had to swallow before she could speak. "Neil has his skipper's licence so they'll hire their own boat. You'll be free to go back to whatever you were doing before I intruded on your life."

He grinned, eyes twinkling. "It's been a very pleasant diversion...so far."

As if she wasn't confused enough. Why did he keep doing that? Making suggestions? Making it sound as though he wanted something more? Last night he'd had *more* on a platter and hadn't taken it.

Rik drifted the boat in on the tide into a different bay from before, where the forest almost seemed to meet the water. While he anchored the sailboat and prepared the dinghy, she retrieved her rucksack and camera, and scanned her checklist one last time. When she returned to the deck, he was re-buttoning his shirt. She swallowed her disappointment.

He closed the last button. "We can return to the boat for lunch, and you can upload your pictures then. What do you still need to photograph?"

"I need a forested area that's penetrable enough for a crew to work in, and a space where they can build a ruin." She climbed down into the waiting dinghy.

"You won't need to build a ruin, there's one already." Rik gunned the outboard motor. "This island wasn't always uninhabited."

It was cooler beneath the trees, and quieter as the constant surge of the ocean receded behind them. Kenzie took off her hat, but wished she could take off more than that. She loved the heat, and had seriously contemplated emigrating somewhere warmer at least a dozen times in her life, but this heat, the kind that burned from the inside out, was seriously uncomfortable.

They tramped through the forest, Rik a few steps ahead as he forged a path through the ferny undergrowth. Kenzie scurried behind, pausing every now and then to snap pictures, but mostly just concentrating on not tripping over the tangled roots at her feet.

Their makeshift path was uphill all the way and her calves were starting to feel it. She almost wished she'd made it to gym any time these last six months.

Nah. Life was too short to waste in a gym. She'd rather be out here trekking through the unexplored wilderness.

Though the view wasn't helping her temperature any. Rik's jeans were fitted enough to give her an unparalleled view of a tautly sculpted ass and muscled thighs. She took a long swig of water from her bottle, but it didn't help. Rik had more than just his torso going for him.

Look, don't touch. Look, don't touch. Touch, don't look.
Damn.

When the ground levelled off, bringing her eye level in line with his shirted back, she was almost disappointed.

"You'll need to send in labour in advance to create paths through this." Rik paused and she nearly smacked into him. He held out a hand to steady her, and another swift rush of blood swept through her. Like she needed any more heating up. She was going to combust any moment.

Focus. This was work, not play. "Won't that destroy the environment?"

"It grows back quickly. Another rainy season and no-one will ever know you were here." He held back the fronds of an over-large fern to let her pass.

"How much further?"

"We're there."

Her eyes grew wide as she looked past him. He hadn't been messing with her. Tumbled down walls of stone peeked out through the foliage. She darted forward, pulling aside the branches and tracing the lines of walls. Not just one ruined building, but a whole settlement. It would need a team of people to clear the underbrush properly, but this was exactly the type of ruin the director wanted.

She prayed her pictures would do the place justice, that he would see this as she could see it beneath the matted vines and ferns.

"Give me the machete," she said, holding out her hand.

Rik frowned. "What for?"

"I need to clear away some of these branches so I can get a decent picture."

"I'll do it. It's a man's job."

She rolled her eyes. Clearly they *did* teach chauvinism in Prince Academy. But she wasn't about to complain. Not when he stripped off his shirt again, giving her an unimpeded view of that magnificent torso gleaming with sweat as he worked. If she were a poet, she'd write a sonnet or two for those biceps. Her fingers itched to capture them on film.

Oh what the heck...

Perhaps Lee would forgive her a little lapse if she brought home a few drool-worthy pictures. She raised her camera.

When he'd cut through a swathe of the overhanging foliage and a corner of one building stood free, Rik stepped back to admire his handiwork. "Will that do?"

She nodded and focussed on her camera. *Will it ever...* "That's perfect. Thanks." The camera shutter whirred again.

Though she didn't need to, she took the folder from her bag and flipped through the printed pictures until she reached a sketch by the storyboard artist. She compared her pictures to the artist's impression. A phenomenal match, down to the bromeliads and orchids in the trees. "This is the place!"

"Yes it is."

But Rik wasn't looking at the page, or at her. His gaze had fallen onto the stretch of wall he'd uncovered in his hasty clearance. He bent down to look at a heart-shaped inscription carved into a corner stone, like a piece of ancient graffiti.

Kenzie bent too. "*TT and CA*. What does it mean?"

He knelt beside the wall and rubbed the inscription reverently. "They were real. And they survived. If only my father..." His voice caught.

Not wanting to touch what she could only imagine was a complicated issue, she asked instead "Who survived?"

"The pirate and his princess."

"From the legend – they were real?"

"Of course. There's a grain of truth in every legend. My father was fascinated by the story and collected every scrap of information he could find. It's well documented that Governor von Kerkhoven lost his bride to a dark-skinned privateer, and in revenge he did his best to rid the Caribbean of pirates. But his bride was a daughter of the Count of Arelat, not a princess, and the jilted groom was no sorcerer, just a man with a small navy at his command. This settlement was only one of the casualties."

"I feel sorry for him," Kenzie said. "Still doesn't mean he had to act out. What happened to the girl?"

"That's always been the mystery. There was no record of either her or the pirate after they eloped. Until now." He stroked his hand over the stone. "Thomas Taylor and Clara d'Arelat. So they survived the legendary battle and lived long enough to leave their mark here."

"This could be a national monument," she suggested. Or a theme park, but that just sounded tacky. Almost as tacky as having a film crew barge through here in a few months' time.

She snapped a few pictures of the inscription. If Rik happened to be in at least half of them, no-one but her need ever know. These pictures were for her alone.

"So is that your work all done?" He rose, wiping grimy hands on his jeans.

"It is. This place is amazing. It's unbelievable that I've found everything on one island: beaches, lagoon, forest. Even the ruins. That'll save the production a few bob rather than having to build a set. I guess we should start making our way back to the boat."

Not that she was in any hurry to leave, even if the hike was downhill all the way, with lunch at the end of it.

***

This was not the way they'd come, Kenzie was sure. The forest seemed denser and less friendly. She'd lost all sense of direction, and the urge to photograph her surroundings had deserted her at least a mile back.

"I don't think we're in Kansas anymore, Toto," she muttered. A hanging vine slapped her in the face, and she came to a halt. "Uh, Rik..."

He paused to look back at her.

"I don't suppose you happen to have a GPS in that rucksack of yours? Or a compass?"

He shrugged. "We don't need a compass. I have an excellent sense of direction."

Yeah, and she had an excellent sense of trouble, but that didn't stop her from plunging headlong into it.

"So you're sure this is the way we came?"

He looked about them, as if noticing their surroundings for the first time. How many miles away had he been?

"It's not the same way, but as long as we're headed downhill, we should reach the beach soon. Then we can follow the shoreline back to the boat."

She hoped so. This was a bloody big island, and her hiking boots were beginning to chafe. Not to mention, her water bottle was empty. And sweat had begun to pour down her back. That look might work on Rik, but on her it didn't look anything like a wet tee shirt contest, she was sure.

He resumed his forward surge and she followed in his wake. The path was more slippery now, mossy beneath their feet, with steep banks and sudden gullies hidden beneath a carpet of waist-high bushes that scratched and tugged at her. Not to mention the vines that dangled from the branches above, like snakes coiled ready to spring.

The canopy overhead was too dense to judge where the sun

was in the sky, but according to her watch it was past lunch time. Her stomach agreed with the watch.

Which would make it the end of a normal working day in London. Not that a production company in full-on pre-production mode would be working normal hours.

The noise of the forest escalated the further they travelled – the call of birds, the rustle of wind in the leaves, and a low roar that seemed to come up through the soles of her feet.

Rik paused and waited for her to catch up. "I think we might be lost."

No kidding. And, typical man, he hadn't believed he needed directions.

Since they were stating the obvious, she added her two cents. "And we're out of fresh water."

"That we may be able to do something about." He cocked his ear and listened. "Follow the sound."

On the plus side, the nearer they got to that low roar, the more the trees thinned out and the patches of dappled light grew bigger and brighter. The forest no longer seemed quite so menacing beneath the cloudless sapphire sky.

Then they emerged into a sunny glade.

Kenzie caught her breath.

There it was, the source of the sound. Amidst the emerald green of the forest, the stark white plume of a waterfall, falling down a rocky shelf into a pool before flowing away downhill.

The air was richly fragrant here, heavy with the scent of wild frangipani flowers run amok. The colours too were vivid: rich greens, the delicate whites and yellows of the flowers, the brilliant flash of red and blue as a macaw skimmed through the treetops.

"Wow – look at this place!" She clambered over the sun-warmed rocks at the waterfall's base to reach the pool. Peering in, she splashed cool water on her face, her neck, her arms. Instant relief.

The water was crystal clear beneath the bubbling surface, and small, bright fish darted through the shallows. Tentatively she cupped a hand in the water and tasted. Unbelievable. Completely fresh and sweet, untainted by human intervention.

She sighed in satisfaction.

She might be lost, she might not have a plan for her life or know where her next pay check was coming from, but right at this moment there wasn't any place she'd rather be than here beside this waterfall, soaking up the scents and sounds and colours.

That feeling was back, the feeling she'd pursued her whole life, the sense of *more* she'd always yearned for. Except it was no longer a yearning. It was right now, right here.

Not a person, or a job, but a place. A place so achingly beautiful that the rest of the world with its petty woes didn't exist. A place where being lost didn't even matter.

Sometimes getting lost was the only way to find oneself. If they hadn't have got lost, they'd never have discovered this waterfall.

Rik squatted beside her, his proximity sending an increasingly familiar frisson of desire and confusion through her.

He bent to fill his water bottle, casting her a sideways glance. "You're all wet." His gaze lingered on her chest and the lace bra that had become visible through the sodden white fabric of her tee shirt.

She splashed him. "Now you are too." She sat back on her haunches. "So what's the plan?"

He grinned. "I thought you weren't big on plans? Aren't you enjoying this adventure?"

"I've had about as much adventure as I can take for one day. My blisters are killing me. If I wasn't deathly terrified of snakes, I'd have taken off my boots and socks long ago."

His grin turned to a smirk. "Then you probably shouldn't turn around right now."

She froze. He was kidding, right?

"You're kidding, right?" she croaked.

He leaned close, his voice low. "Don't move."

She didn't. She couldn't.

He leaned even closer, so close his breath tickled her ear. "Just kidding," he whispered.

"Jerk!" she pushed his chest, all her adrenalin and anger and sexual frustration bubbling together. She pushed harder than she intended. Rik sprawled backwards into the pool.

She didn't bother to hide her laughter, but she was so busy laughing that when he lunged for her, she wasn't quick enough. He pulled her down into the water, on top of him.

His lungs forgot to breathe. Rik looped an arm around her waist and held her close. Her body moulded to his, sparking sensation wherever they touched. He was amazed the water didn't start to boil around them.

He'd thought of nothing but kissing her for two excruciating, maddening days. This was his moment. They were truly alone. No chance of a paparazzi camera or mobile phone in miles, as there'd been at the resort last night.

Kenzie looked up at him through her long fringe of ginger hair, turned to red-gold in the sunlight. His fingers itched to stroke the hair back from her face. He felt something he'd never felt before, something primal and violent and unstoppable. Desire. Passion. He didn't feel like a prince or a ruler or a hopeless drifter. He felt like a man. And he wanted to do what every man wanted to do with a beautiful woman.

Her pupils were so large, so dark, that they swallowed her irises. He traced a finger down the curve of her cheek, coming to rest on her lips.

But in the second he hesitated, she blinked as if waking from a trance, and pulled away. "Oh no! I'm not falling for that again!"

What the hell did that mean? He frowned.

She splashed to the pool's edge, and climbed out onto a rock, so massive it was more ledge than rock. She unlaced her hiking boots and removed her socks to let them dry in the sun.

He moved to perch beside her and did the same. They sat side by side, clothes dripping and bare feet trailing in the blessedly cool water. Birdsong and the waterfall's roar filled the pregnant silence.

He leaned back on his elbows and studied her. She was flushed again. Not from the heat, but that delicate shade of pink she turned whenever she blushed.

He wanted to kiss her more than he wanted to breathe, and it was obvious she felt the attraction too. So why did she resist?

What was it about him she didn't like?

This was new terrain for him. As a prince, he'd had to be extremely careful whom he slept with, yet he'd never had a problem finding willing women. And he'd certainly never struggled to understand them before as he struggled to understand Kenzie.

It was a horribly lowering thought that perhaps he'd never been particularly likeable. Perhaps he'd only been loved for his title and not for himself.

"I wonder if Thomas and Clara ever came here? This is the perfect place to fall in love, isn't it?" Kenzie's babble pulled him back from that dark place he was growing far too familiar with.

"I wouldn't know. I've never been in love."

Kenzie faced him, eyes widening in surprise. "You've got to be at least thirty four or thirty five. How can you never have been in love?"

"And you have?"

"Of course. Several times. I was madly in love with all my boyfriends in the beginning."

"How many boyfriends have you had?"

She counted on both hands. "Three. How many have you had?"

He laughed. "I've never had any boyfriends."

"Okay then – how many serious *girlfriends* have you had?"

What constituted serious? Someone he'd given more than a passing thought to when she wasn't in his bed? He pretended to count on both hands before he looked up at Kenzie. "One. And I planned to marry her." Even though she was the one woman he'd dated who he hadn't slept with.

Kenzie screwed up her face. "I thought you said you'd never been in love."

"What does love have to do with marriage? Since you've no doubt fallen *out* of love with all of those boyfriends you were 'madly in love with,' surely you must know passionate love doesn't last?"

He'd had enough time to reflect on this these last few months. That last night in the castle at Waldburg, when he'd faced his mother and demanded the truth, had only confirmed his beliefs. She had confessed to being wildly in love with his father. Not Christian, Archduke of Westerwald, but some fashion photographer she'd met in New York.

But the photographer hadn't wanted her. She'd been just another random conquest to him. When her manager suggested marriage to a prince, the heir to a European Archduchy, she'd jumped at the chance to get away, to start afresh. She hadn't known she was pregnant until after she'd arrived in Westerwald, and by then it had been too late to back out. So she'd passed off her bastard child as another man's.

They'd had a happy marriage, Rik knew that. But it had been a marriage of convenience not of passion. Passion didn't last. Love didn't last. Only mutual convenience did.

"You might be right." Kenzie worried her lower lip. "So let me get this straight: you've only ever had one girlfriend, who you weren't in love with, and you don't do one-night stands? Are you sure you're even into women?"

Moments ago she'd had his erection pressed against her stomach as he'd been about to kiss her, and she still doubted him? He raised an eyebrow. "Do I seem gay to you?"

"My gaydar's usually pretty good, but I'm always open to being proved wrong." Her next words were spoken so softly, he nearly missed them: "It would be easier if you were."

"I'm not gay. I like women." The tightness of his jeans right now was proof enough of that.

True, there'd been remarkably few women over the years who'd made the grade. He'd left the womanising to Max. As the older brother, the heir, he'd always had to be more circumspect. It didn't look good for a future Archduke to change partners too often. And he certainly couldn't risk sleeping with anyone who might sell her story to the media. The kind of women who were attracted to the limelight usually weren't the kind of women who made suitable Archduchess material. He'd only met one who'd been truly suitable.

Teresa had been raised to be a princess. She was intelligent, she knew how to behave, came from an impeccable lineage, and nothing fazed her. Best of all, she was a woman who did not allow her passions to rule her.

She deserved to be a princess, and he hoped for her sake she still would be…though Europe was rapidly running out of eligible princes.

One thing was certain – that door had closed for him. It was just another piece of his well-ordered life that had crumbled to dust. No-one was going to wave a magic wand, erase the past and make him a prince again. There was no going back, and there was no point dwelling on what he'd lost. That much he'd learned these past few months. He shrugged off the dark thoughts, and grinned as Kenzie's stomach made an audible rumble.

"Until we get back to the boat, how about some mangoes to stave off the hunger pains?" Without waiting for her assent, he got to his feet and climbed across the rocks to the far side of the clearing. Beneath the mango tree, over-ripe fruit lay scattered in the grass, bruised and broken, but on the branches above he managed to find a few pieces the birds and monkeys hadn't got to yet. He returned to Kenzie's side with his hands full.

She reached eagerly for one of the bright yellow mangoes and bit into it. Juice dribbled down her chin. She attempted to lick it, her small pink tongue darting over her lips. His chest pulled tight. God, he wanted to kiss that mouth, to take possession of it, so badly it almost hurt.

She bit into the mango again, and his mouth watered.

"Don't do that," he warned.

"Don't do what?" She widened her eyes in mock innocence, but the wicked twinkle gave her away. "This?" She licked her lips again, slowly, deliberately. Damn her, she knew what it was doing to him. "What will you do to me?"

Their gazes held for a breathless moment.

"I'm going to do what I should have done in that pool earlier. And this time I'm not going to let you slip away."

She lifted the mango to her mouth and took a slow, playful nip, her gaze never wavering from his.

His stomach tightened as his blood rushed south. He leaned towards her, his mouth closing over hers. Her lips were soft but firm, and she tasted sweet and exotic. He traced his tongue over her lips, licking the mango juice from her skin.

She moaned.

And the spark between them ignited.

Rik pulled her into his arms, hard against him, crushing her mouth with his. She opened up for him and he dived in, exploring, demanding, consuming.

Her arms wrapped around his waist, clinging to him as he kissed her mouth.

She had to know the effect she was having on him, had to feel his erection growing hard and insistent between them. But this time she didn't pull away, didn't fight him.

He didn't know what had changed for her, and he didn't care. He rolled onto her, supporting himself on either side of her with his elbows, edging her thighs apart with his knee. She moaned again, arching against him, pressing firm beasts into his chest, and the warm, molten heat of her core against his throbbing erection.

His hands slid beneath her tee shirt, skating over cool, smooth skin. His own body was on fire. It consumed him.

He'd never known such a savage kiss, a kiss that crossed the line from seduction into madness.

So this was how passion felt.

He only broke the kiss when they were both breathless. He sank his head into her shoulder and breathed in her subtle perfume, a sweet scent that reminded him of orange blossoms.

In that kiss he'd felt as if the last shred of the person he'd been, those last pieces of himself he'd clung to had shattered and blew away on the wind. And in its place only one thing was left: hope.

Chapter Seven

She could have carried on kissing him all day and all night. But for a change, Kenzie's brain overruled her impulses. She pulled away from Rik, breathing heavily.

His grip on her waist tightened. "I said I wasn't going to let you slip away again."

"We need to get out of here before dark and I need to send my pictures before the London office closes for the night."

He let her go, slowly, reluctantly, though his eyes were still hooded with desire. It was a tad disconcerting to see a man with Rik's control, his lack of emotion, abandon himself so entirely. It was also rather heady to know she was the one who'd brought him over to the dark side.

Resisting the urge to pick up where they'd left off, she cleared her throat. "Water flows downhill to the sea, right?" she asked, pulling on her socks and boots. They were uncomfortably damp still. "So if we follow this river, we should reach the beach."

He nodded and began to pull on his own socks and shoes.

With their water bottles re-filled, they followed the river as it tumbled downhill. In places the undergrowth was so tangled they had to walk in the water. The river was swift-flowing but low enough in this dry season not to be dangerous, yet the rocks were still slippery and they made slow progress.

Though the sun was now over the yardarm, the air seemed even hotter, without a hint of breeze. Almost as though the world was holding its breath.

"It's still several weeks until the rainy season," Rik said, taking her hand to help her scramble up the riverbank. "But this weather feels like there's a storm brewing."

In more ways than one. Inside, she felt as though there was a hurricane that threatened to break through her skin at any moment. She'd been in lust before, even more often than she'd been in love, but this was something else, something even more powerful that she couldn't name.

It scared her. It thrilled her.

Once they found the boat and returned to Los Pajaros she should say *goodbye* and *thank you* and walk away. But she wouldn't. That kiss had changed everything.

The jungle grew less dense, and they were able to leave the riverbed and walk along the banks. Rik still held her hand.

The sun baked down between the trees, no cooler than it had been at midday. Her shirt was plastered to her body, and her hair clung limply to her face. This humidity wasn't conducive to fighting one's way through a forest.

For about thirty seconds during Rik's kiss she'd felt as sexy as a Hollywood goddess. That feeling was history. It was impossible to feel sexy with a red face, aching calves in damp shoes, and sweat trickling down between her breasts.

The moment when the forest trees gave way to palm trees, and the earth turned sandy beneath her feet, Kenzie could have knelt down and kissed the ground. This wasn't the bay where they'd moored the yacht, but she didn't care. She wasn't lost any more.

"Thank you God," she prayed. She shucked off her boots and socks, and dug her bare toes into the warm, silky sand. Bliss.

This bay was a perfect crescent of incandescent white sand edging a wide lagoon of the clearest, most inviting translucent turquoise. Coconut palms, their broad leaves glossy yellow-green in the afternoon light, lined the beach. This was the bay they'd recommended for filming the pirate ship. Salvatore Lagoon, she'd named it, after the film's hero. And a salvation it had indeed turned out to be.

"You need suntan lotion," Rik observed, rummaging in his rucksack.

She shook her head. "No, what I need is a swim."

"You brought a swimsuit?"

Who needed a swimsuit? At this point she'd be willing to go in fully clothed if it meant she could wash off the sweat and grime of the long hike.

But she had a better idea. She lifted her tee shirt over her head, smiling a little as she heard Rik suck in a breath. Then she pulled her hair band from her hair, dropping it onto her shirt on the ground. Her hair fell loose about her shoulders.

She unbuckled her belt and stepped out of her cargo pants. She didn't look at Rik. She didn't need to look to know what effect her striptease was having. The electricity sparking in the air told her enough.

Dressed only in bra and knickers, she made a mad dash for the sea before she could chicken out.

She paused a moment at the water's edge, the salty seawater stinging the blisters on her heels. The water pulled away, leaving her feet embedded in soft sand. She wriggled her toes free and waded in deeper, enticed by the near-forgotten thrill of waves licking at her bare limbs. The cool caress of the water outweighed any sting.

She'd been in the Caribbean for days and hadn't once swum in the sea. How sad was that?

The gentle waves, white-crested and foaming, invited her in. She dived, and water closed over her head.

She stayed under for as long as she could hold her breath before she surfaced, spraying droplets in all directions as she broke the surface.

"Better?" Rik asked, wading through waist-deep water towards her. He'd removed his clothes too, and the sight of him, dripping wet and unnervingly predatory, took what was left of her breath away. The sunlight gleamed off his broad, tanned shoulders, making it appear as though the inked dragon was alive and breathing.

"Much."

Her breathing jump-started, but now her heart was beating wildly against her sternum. He was so close she only had to reach out to lay her hand on the hard-packed muscle of his stomach.

The memory of his kiss prickled at her lips.

"We're not lost any more." His voice sounded rough.

"I know."

The water rushed like silk between her legs as a wave swept around them, pushing them closer together. He stooped to pick her up and lifted her clear off her feet. Without thinking, she wrapped her legs around his waist, feeling weightless in the water.

"And we have nowhere else to be..." His voice abraded her cheek.

Strictly speaking, she should be on the boat, uploading today's photographs. If the director liked what she'd found today, Neil needed to book flights first thing in the morning. As with all film shoots, prep time was short, and the race wasn't over until she'd sold the team on Tortuga.

She buried her head in Rik's neck and breathed him in. Her lips grazed his neck, tasting the salt of the sea.

She shouldn't get distracted now. She should get out of Rik's arms right now. The clock was ticking.

Sod the clock! And sod what she should and shouldn't do.

There was something important she *needed* to do first.

She tilted her head back, raised her face and closed her eyes. This time she wasn't disappointed. His mouth crushed hers, possessive, demanding, and she was really glad he was holding her up as there was no way she would be able to stand on her own two feet.

Rik's beard tickled her skin; surprisingly softer than the abrasive stubble she'd expected. His hands roved over her back as he deepened the kiss, sending skitters of sensation up and down her spine. The ripples radiated outwards, pooling in the juncture of her thighs. She rubbed herself against him, needing to ease the growing torment between her legs.

Through the thin fabric of her soaking wet knickers, his hardness pressed against her. Her stomach contracted. Oh lordy...he must have been commando beneath those jeans.

He was completely naked now.

There was nothing but the teensiest piece of cotton separating them.

Her nipples hardened beneath the wet, scratchy lace of her bra. As if sensing her need, his large hand rounded over her breast, his fingers sliding beneath the lace. He tugged and teased her taut nipple until she throbbed with unmet need.

She was way beyond the help of any cold shower. She wanted to come, and she wanted to come with Rik inside her.

She begged him not to stop, begged him to give her relief. His mouth skirted down her neck, over her collarbone, and closed over her nipple. He sucked through the translucent fabric of the wet bra. She arched her back, pushing up her breasts, and moaned as the sensation struck right to her core.

Her moan was all he needed. His hand slid over her hip, her thigh, between their bodies, sending a spasm of pleasure rocketing through her as his fingers touched her clit. He stroked her, nipping her peaked nipple with his teeth as she moaned again.

"Tell me you want me to stop," he said.

Was he mad? She couldn't stop now. And she'd kill him if he even tried to stop.

But she couldn't speak, couldn't answer, as he slid his finger inside her. She writhed against him, wanting more, and he pushed deeper. He had to know she wasn't just wet from the sea water.

"Are you ready? I don't want to hurt you." He sounded breathless.

"Making me wait is hurting me."

He yanked her knickers roughly aside, and her blood pounded

between her ears in anticipation. With one arm still clamped around her waist, holding her to him, he lowered her onto his erection.

He filled her, stretched her, and she cried out. Then she thrust her hips forward, pulling him in. The surge of the waves rocked them together, echoing their motion as Rik retreated then drove back into her. She rocked with him, forcing him deeper with every plunge, breathtaking pleasure spiralling through her, building, rising, until she couldn't think, until nothing existed but the slide of him inside her and her own ecstasy.

Then she tumbled over that delicious precipice and fireworks exploded inside her head. Rik's climax followed her own as he let himself go.

She sank her head against his shoulder, both body and mind spent. He slid out of her and the salt water rushed between them.

And that was when reality hit.

They hadn't used protection.

They stood for a long moment, hearts thumping wildly together, the waves still breaking against them, her legs still wound around his waist. She breathed him in, all salty sea tang and wild masculinity.

Was it worth the risk ? The slide of skin on skin, feeling him inside her without any barrier... yes, Kenzie decided, that was worth a moment's danger. And he'd made it clear he didn't do this often. He was a prince.

She unclamped her legs from his waist, readying herself to stand on her own, but Rik grasped her tighter. He laughed, a low, sensual rumble, his throat vibrating against her mouth. "There's no danger of us getting caught in the forest after dark now, and this time I'm not letting you go."

Still carrying her, he waded clear out of the water, up the beach to the shade of the palms where he'd laid out a thin plastic ground sheet from his rucksack. The slanting sun turned the beach golden, or maybe that was just her own afterglow.

He laid her down on her back on the groundsheet, and knelt over her. The sheet wasn't soft and it wasn't pretty, but Kenzie didn't give a damn. If it kept sand out of delicate places, she was happy.

She laid a hand on his chest, holding him back, taking a moment to savour the view of him. She'd imagined him naked. The reality exceeded her wildest imagination. He was all solid strength and male beauty, his chest smooth and hairless, like a teen magazine centrefold. She tentatively reached up to touch the dragon tattoo that curved over his shoulder, tracing the dragon's tail down his arm.

His erection shifted, and she smiled. She wouldn't have to wait long for a repeat performance. He lowered himself onto her, pressing between her legs.

But. She bit her lip, fighting her rising need for him. "Rik..."

"Mmm?" he bent his head closer to flick his tongue across her lips.

She ducked her head away. Once might not tempt fate, but a second time...

"We can't do this," she managed.

His brow furrowed as he pulled away to look at her. "We just did."

She swallowed. "We don't have any protection."

His face froze as he took in her words. "Oh my God."

Her sentiments exactly.

Slowly, carefully, he lifted himself off her and dragged in a breath. "We're not lost anymore. We're about a mile's walk from where we left the boat. And I have condoms on the boat. Do you think you can make it?"

Of course she could make it. She could climb mountains to get to those condoms. Hell, she would fly, if she needed to.

He stood and held out a hand to help her up. She took his outstretched hand, and when he pulled her up, he pulled her against him. Their bodies met, their mouths met.

"We'd better get dressed." His cheek rasped against hers. She nodded.

They dressed quickly, and in silence. When she tried to tie her hair back into a ponytail, he stopped her hand.

"Leave it loose." He stroked his fingers through the damp strands. "You have beautiful hair."

When they were dressed, and the groundsheet had been folded back into the rucksack, they began the hike along the forest line, heading for the bay where they'd moored the yacht. Rik twined his fingers through hers and held her hand as they walked. Not even blisters or hunger could stop her now.

As the sun angled down across the sky, and a cool sea breeze caressed her skin dry, a little of her sanity returned. She still hadn't uploaded her day's pictures to the office in London. She glanced at her watch.

It was gone four o'clock. Which made it...she gave up on the mental calculation of London-time. It made it late London-time. And though film production people were notorious for working all hours, if she didn't get her pictures there *now*...

What if the director chose to visit the Virgin Islands instead? Then this would all have been for nothing... no, perhaps not nothing. The stroke of Rik's hand across her palm sent a dazzling glow through her, reminding her that this trip had been good for at least one thing.

He held her hand all the way back, right up until they reached the beach where they'd left the dinghy.

The little boat had floated halfway out to sea. Rik swore. "The tide must have carried it out while we were lost."

The yacht seemed a whole lot further away than she remembered. Impossible to reach without a boat – and certainly not while carrying an expensive camera.

"It's going to be hours before the tide washes the dinghy back in," Rik said.

She swallowed, and though her first thought was '*the condoms are on that boat*', what she said was: "I need to upload my pictures to London."

She sank down on the strip of beach which had more than doubled in size since they'd passed through that morning.

This was just bloody typical of her life. One step forward, two steps back.

Impossibly hot, indulgent sex with a prince on a tropical beach, followed by being marooned on a deserted island with everything you wanted and needed just tantalisingly out of reach. She was getting really, really tired of always needing a back up plan. Just once, wouldn't it be nice if everything worked out first time around?

Chapter Eight

Kenzie's shoulders sagged for barely a moment before she lifted her chin, the determined look returning to her face. Rik admired her tenacity. She never gave up, never let defeat drag her down.

Not the way he had.

This was his fault. He'd checked the tide tables and planned to have them back at the boat before the tide turned. They'd only got lost because he'd drifted back into the past instead of paying attention to where they were headed. Looking back to the past caused nothing but grief.

The dinghy had to be a good mile out. And this cove was less protected than the others since the break in the reef offered no defence against the wild ocean here. These were no gently lapping waves, but crashing breakers, battered by the wind that whipped beyond the shelter of the bay.

Still, he'd swum through worse. Though at the time, admittedly, he hadn't cared if he drowned.

Before he'd met Kenzie and rediscovered what it felt like to be alive.

He stripped off his jeans and shirt. He seemed to be making a habit of that around her. "I guess I'll have to swim for it then."

She turned a startled gaze on him. "Is that wise?"

95

Who cared about 'wise?' He'd spent his whole life being rational and careful, and he was sick of it. Where had caution ever got him?

Kissing Kenzie, making love to her...for the first time in his life he'd followed his instincts and let passion overrule his reason. And it had felt good.

He would trust his instincts again now.

Without answering, he dove into the waves, and began to plough through them. They battered at him, rolled over him and submerged him, but he relished the fight. He'd left Westerwald without a fight, running away into the night because he'd believed a clean break would be better for his nation.

A person is not defeated when they lose, a person is only defeated when they quit. That had been another of his father's favourite sayings. He was over quitting. From now on he was going to fight for what he wanted. Starting with getting Kenzie safely onto the yacht where she could get her work done... and after that, she was his. No interruptions, no excuses, and a box full of condoms.

He'd never had sex without protection before. He'd always been so careful – princes couldn't afford accidents. But today he'd been so caught up in the moment, in the emotion, he hadn't even given it a thought until Kenzie pointed it out. How could he be such a fool? Especially now he knew he was one of those 'accidents'.

It had felt good, though. Stupid, but good.

He stroked through the waves, fighting the current that pulled at him as he pushed through. Every morning he swam, pitting himself against the elements. Out here in the open sea he'd discovered the purest form of oblivion. There was no other thought but survival, of conquering the elemental force of the water. No time for memory or regret or despair.

In spite of the rougher water, of the churning waves that surged over him, under him, in a violent caress, this swim was even better. It felt good to simply be alive. For too many months he'd done nothing but exist, wanting only the things that were denied to him. Now at last he'd found something he wanted, and he wasn't going to quit until he got it. Again and again and again.

He swam until his legs ached, until his chest throbbed with the effort of drawing in air.

The wave carrying him crested and broke, and in that moment he glimpsed the dinghy. It was mere metres away. The outgoing tide pulled at him, threatening to sweep him further away. With his breath burning in his chest, he poured every last ounce of fight left in him to reach the little boat. His hands stretched out for the vessel which rocked violently on the breakers, crashing down another metre further away. He'd have sworn if that hadn't meant a lungful of seawater.

He plunged forward, and gripped the boat's side. For a moment he clung, too spent to drag himself out of the water and into the boat.

Then another wave crashed over him and his fingers began to slip. Involuntarily, he opened his mouth to gasp, and water rushed in, choking him. For the first time it occurred to him he might drown. And Kenzie would be alone on an island no local dared set foot upon.

He'd be damned before he let a stupid curse keep him from what he wanted. Tortuga was not going to get the better of him.

His grasp tightened and he heaved himself out of the water and into the boat.

For a dizzying moment he lay in the bottom of the dinghy, coughing and gasping for breath. Thank God for all the swimming he'd done these past months. When he'd been a soft prince living in a palace, waited on hand and foot, he'd never have managed this feat.

He thought of Kenzie, on the beach, anxiously waiting for him, watching for him, and pulled himself upright. Wiping the dripping water from his face, he rose shakily in the pitching boat. It took two attempts to get the engine fired up, then he turned the boat back towards shore.

Within the shelter of the bay, the waves smoothed out and

the dinghy skimmed across the water. The white sliver of beach seemed impossibly far, and he pushed the dinghy faster, following an overwhelming urge to reach dry land. For this once, the shore wasn't the place where reality waited for him like an ominous shadow. It was where he wanted to be. It was the place where Kenzie waited for him.

She waded out to meet him, cradling her camera bag like a baby. The relief on her face was gratifying. "You're sopping wet."

"Water tends to do that."

She handed him the camera bag and returned to the beach to fetch his clothes and the rucksacks, then climbed into the boat beside him. "I lost sight of you for a while. You had me scared."

"You would have been okay. You're resourceful like that."

She clouted him. "Don't be a dolt. It was you I was scared for."

He swallowed against the lump in his throat. It was nice to have someone who cared. He'd felt alone for far too long.

When they reached the yacht, drifting placidly on its mooring as though absolutely nothing had happened, he was so depleted he could barely climb the swim ladder onto the deck. Without comment, Kenzie stowed her camera bag and helped him secure the dinghy.

"I'll get you something to eat," she said, her brow furrowed in concern.

"Send your pictures first."

"Screw the pictures."

Kenzie not only had a kind heart. She was fierce in her defence of anything and anyone she cared about. Despite her fragile build and too-young face, she was a stronger, better woman than he'd given her credit for that first night.

He took her arm and propelled her towards the cabin. "Food can wait. Send your pictures," he commanded.

She nodded meekly, the usual flash of defiance noticeably absent from her eyes, and that alone spoke volumes of how frightened she'd been.

In the yacht's tiny bathroom, smaller than any wardrobe he'd ever owned, he stood under the shower until the water ran cold. Then he pulled on the spare sweater and chinos he kept on board and returned to the saloon where Kenzie had thrown together a meal.

He frowned at her. "Have you sent your pictures?"

She nodded, pushing her long fringe back from her face. "Neil will probably call as soon as they've viewed them."

He grinned. "Luckily for us, there isn't a mobile tower in sight. He'll have to leave a message." He chose not to mention the satellite phone on board.

They ate in silence, the air between them humming with delicious tension. His body was no longer tired, and in spite of the ache in his limbs, he was hard again.

He shoved his plate aside and rose, needing something to take the edge off his desire. This time he wanted to take it slowly. He wanted to give her pleasure. Not come like a schoolboy with no self-control as he had in the ocean.

He found a bottle of white wine in the little fridge. A glance at the label and his heart pulled tight. It was one of Max's Californian wines.

He poured two glasses and held one out to Kenzie, his fingers lingering over hers on the crystal stem as she took it. Her gaze met his, her eyes clouded with desire.

He drank a long draught of the wine then held out his other hand to her. Without question she took it and he pulled her to her feet. Then he led her to the aft cabin.

The low ceilinged room had not been designed for comfort, and though the bed stretched from wall to wall, it wasn't nearly big enough. But until he could get her back to the villa and the luxury of his own bed, this would have to do.

He set down his glass on the narrow shelf above the bed, and sat on the edge, pulling her to stand between his legs. She came willingly, with a wicked smile and a smouldering look in her eyes that made his blood boil.

She bent her head to kiss him, her hair falling around him in a cascade of soft tresses. He threaded his fingers through it, holding it back from her face, and eased his tongue between her lips, into the soft wet warmth of her mouth. His body ached to sink into the soft wet warmth between her legs too, but he held himself back, even though it took every ounce of effort left in him not to tumble her onto her back.

He broke their kiss to yank her shirt over her head. Her white lacy bra had dried, and was no longer see-through. With one hand he unclasped it, and she shrugged out of it, revealing perfect breasts. His hands already knew their shape, but his body tightened at the sight of her nipples, pink and tightly budded.

He removed the wine glass held limply in her hand and dipped his fingers into the golden liquid, then trailed his wet fingers between her breasts, over the soft mounds, tracing circles. He licked at first one, then the other, and she shivered.

He sucked her nipple into his mouth, savouring the taste of her, that faint essence of orange blossoms beneath the taste of the wine, a stimulating combination of innocence and impishness.

He playfully bit her, his teeth grazing the erect bud, and she let out a soft cry. There was nothing innocent about Kenzie beneath that delicate skin. He knew she liked it rough. She liked it hard.

And as he was slowly discovering, so did he.

He stripped off her cargo pants and knickers, and she stood naked before him. He sighed his pleasure. He stroked a hand through her pale curls, and she parted her legs, inviting him in.

He withdrew his hand, not touching her as she wanted, making her wait.. Her eyes flew open and she frowned.

He held the wine glass to her lips and let her drink, then took a long sip himself. Then he flipped her onto her back on the bed and poured the dregs of the wine between her legs. He slid down the bed between her thighs, parting her with his fingers.

Kenzie gasped as his mouth closed over her. He licked down her, sucking up the droplets of wine that clung to her sensitive skin.

It was killing him taking this so slowly, and his chinos pulled painfully tightly, but he wanted her to enjoy this. Wanted her to remember this day and how he'd made her feel long after they went their separate ways.

His tongue teased her. He nipped and kissed her clit, until she cried out; until she came in a series of tiny shocks that shook her entire body. Only when she lay limply on the bed, breathing heavily, did he rise and strip off his own clothes.

Then he stretched out above her on the bed, holding his weight off her with his arms. "Tell me you want this."

She nodded.

"Tell me."

She laughed, a low, husky sound. "You want me to beg?"

"Well, that would be nice."

Her eyes gleamed with mischief. "Please, sir, may I have some more?" She arched her back, rubbing herself up against him. "And this time, don't forget the rubber."

As if. Much as he wanted to feel her skin against his again, that wasn't a mistake he would make twice.

He retrieved the box of condoms from the shelf above the bed, removed one and ripped the foil packet open with his teeth. Kenzie took the condom, 'ribbed for her pleasure' according to the box, and rolled it onto him. The firm, heated touch of her hands wrapped around his cock sent a shudder through him.

She stroked down his length, with practiced hands that seemed to know just how he liked it. The pressure built inside him, demanding release, and he had to yank her hand away. He was on the verge of turning into that over-excited schoolboy again.

Nudging her legs further apart, he sank down onto her, enjoying the way she pressed up against him, not afraid to demand what she wanted. Even through the desensitising condom he could feel how wet she was, how ready. He massaged himself over her, teasing her again. Her eyes glazed over with that same desperate expression, the half excited, half afraid look he'd seen in them a dozen times over the last two days.

She wanted him with the same desperation he felt for her. But she still didn't want to feel this way. Something primal and possessive took hold of him.

Last night, looking at her laid out on the bench in his cockpit, so sensual, so relaxed, that silky dress riding up her long pale thighs... he'd felt savage. It had taken every ounce of his precious self-control to play the gentleman and walk away.

He didn't feel gentlemanly now either. Perhaps he had more of his biological father in him than he realised, but the urge to ravage Kenzie was starting to drive him insane.

He wanted to drive away her doubts and her fears and make her want him with every fibre of her being, holding nothing back.

"Please, Rik," she begged, rubbing herself against him. "Please."

He took mercy on her, on himself, sinking himself inside her in one long, ferocious thrust which she met with a thrust of her own. There was no taking it slowly after that. Her moans drove him wild as he drove into her, faster, harder, until years of self-control, of denial, cracked apart and he lost himself in her.

When he came, in a vicious climax that affected every part of him, it was a hundred times more powerful than their first kiss had been. He collapsed onto her, chest heaving, body still shaking. But his soul soared.

He rolled over, pulling Kenzie with him, cradling her against his chest, burying his face in the vivid hair that splayed across his chest. He pulled a blanket over them, staving off the inevitable chill as their sweat-slicked skin cooled.

Then he gave in to the bone-melting post-coital relaxation. He couldn't ever remember feeling so light, so free from tension.

It was as though he'd been only half alive before now. As though in making love to Kenzie he'd finally shed a weight he'd carried for so long. As though he'd finally found himself. And what he'd found wasn't the dutiful son, the straight A student or the diligent prince, but the man he was meant to be.

***

They slept deeply, limbs entwined, bodies rocking together as the boat rolled lazily on the groundswell of the incoming tide. When he woke, stretching muscles cramped and sore from his struggle against the ocean, Kenzie was already stirring beside him. She looked up at him through heavily hooded eyes.

"We should head back to Los Pajaros," he said, brushing her hair back from her face. "You need to get back in range of a mobile signal."

"I feel like I don't ever want to leave Tortuga," she said drowsily.

He didn't either.

He'd only ever been interested in the old legend of the curse of Tortuga in an intellectual way. It had felt like a story in need of an ending. Like his father - the man he'd called father rather than the womanising sperm donor - he'd wondered what end Thomas and Clara had met.

Now he saw the story in a whole new light. He could imagine how Thomas had felt, bringing his pale European beauty to Tortuga, being able to have his way with her at last. His desperation to get her away before another man could lay hands on her, his need to submerge his body in hers and lose himself in her.

No matter how short a time those star-crossed lovers had together before the tropical storm or the governor's revenge ended their idyll, he knew now they'd been happy. Because at least they'd had this.

And now he had too.

"We don't have to leave straight away. We can take what's left of the food and have a picnic on the beach before we leave."

She smiled, eyes lighting up. "But this time we make damn sure the dinghy is safe."

He wasn't going to argue with that.

One of the greatest advantages of a deserted island, Rik discovered, was that clothing was entirely optional. He pulled on his jeans, and Kenzie wore nothing but knickers and his fresh shirt which hung almost to her knees. Barefoot, they walked back along the now familiar sandy path through the forest fringe to the beach at Salvatore Bay, taking their time, stopping as they walked to sneak kisses.

Kissing a beautiful woman really was one of life's greatest pleasures. There were an infinite number of ways to kiss, from the light and playful to the deep and passionate. Never before had he found a woman capable of delivering everything in one mind-blowing kiss though.

They missed the sunset completely, emerging from the trees just as the sun dipped beneath the horizon. The air was blessedly cooler, though the sand retained the day's warmth. The sky still shone with ambient light but the shadows lengthened.

Rik spread out the groundsheet from his rucksack at the base of a palm. They sat and ate, watching the moon rise over the sea, casting an arc of white light across the darkening beach.

When they were done, and even the last of the mangoes were gone, he leaned back against the tree trunk and pulled Kenzie between his legs, her back against his chest, his arm looped loosely around her.

"If you still don't want to go back, we could sleep right here on the beach," he offered.

She could have no idea what a big deal this was for him. He'd never slept anywhere but on the finest linen, never done anything so unplanned, so out of his comfort zone. He'd still prefer the fine linen of his bed to the rough scratch of beach sand, but he wanted to make her happy. And he didn't want this moment to end either.

Kenzie sat up suddenly. "The sand is moving. Look!"

He turned his head. The sand close by was indeed shifting,

rippling and bubbling in a gradually widening circle. "Get back," he whispered urgently, recognising the signs. "It's a turtle hatching."

Moving as quickly and carefully as they could, they grabbed the sheet and their picnic things and retreated several feet to watch in fascination as a small circular depression appeared at the heart of the shifting patch.

"Sleeping on the beach might not be such a good idea after all," he said. "We don't want to disturb any other possible nests."

She nodded slowly. "Let's stay to watch."

"It could take a while."

She raised an eyebrow. "Do we have anything better to do right now?"

He could think of a few things. Most involved getting Kenzie naked again. But this was a once in a lifetime opportunity for her.

He'd been lucky enough to witness a few hatchings over the years, and the sight still moved him every time.

So he folded up the groundsheet and laid it down a safe distance from the nest, and drew Kenzie back into the cocoon of his arms. Then, in awed silence they kept a vigil.

The minutes ticked by with little to see but the writhing beach sand, until at last a dark flat head broke the surface. The tiny turtle peeked through, its head followed by a pair of flippers struggling against the sand.

He recognised the paler markings edging the dark carapace. "It's a green turtle. They're highly endangered since many of their nesting grounds have been taken over by man."

He felt a kinship to the sea turtles that nested here. Isla Tortuga was as much a haven for them as it was for him, the one place that hadn't been taken away from them.

Perhaps he could persuade the mayor to divert a little of the film's funds to turning the island into a protected sanctuary? Though there wasn't much need to protect it since no one came here anyway. No one but him, until now.

But too soon a film crew of hundreds would descend on this

island, and it would no longer be his secret. There were researchers who'd probably kill to get access to the island's untouched flora and fauna, and divers who'd pay small fortunes to explore the wrecks. If they discovered that the ban on Tortuga was lifted…

The island would need someone to protect it, someone to care for it.

"Take my camera," Kenzie whispered, thrusting her camera at him. "I don't want to miss any of this, but we should have pictures for posterity."

Rik had usually been on the other end of a camera, but it didn't take a genius to figure out how to work the thing. He zoomed in and focussed just as a second head pushed up beneath the first.

Suddenly there were dozens of baby turtles, shoving and crawling over each other to climb out the hole, spilling up and out like oil from a well, their tiny bodies dark against the pale sand. The most intrepid raced ahead in a straight line towards the edge of the water as more and more poured from the hole.

Rik snapped away, fiddling with the camera controls to compensate for the fading light, his pulse racing as he caught image after image. The turtles motored across the cooling sand in a rapid, ungainly gait until they reached the water where they gave up the fight and let the waves sweep them away.

The last turtles emerged covered in clinging wet sand, flailing to climb from the ever widening, deepening hole, until there was only one turtle remaining.

In his struggle to claw up the steep bank of the collapsing hole, he flipped onto his back, limbs flailing.

"Should we help him?" Kenzie whispered urgently.

He stifled a laugh. "Have patience. It'll all work out in the end." He heard a faint echo to his words and frowned. Then shrugging off the eerie feeling, he focussed his attention back on the camera and watched as the struggling turtle managed to right itself, clawed out of the hole, and chased towards the moonlit sea in the wake of the others. Kenzie cheered quietly.

The waves continued to lap in on the beach, silent and deserted now, the shadowy hole in the sand the only disturbance.

"Whew." Kenzie sagged back against him. "That was truly an awesome sight."

A vastly over-rated word *awesome*, but just this once he agreed.

He handed her the camera so she could examine the pictures he'd taken. She flicked through them. "Wow – these are good. Have you done a lot of photography?"

He shrugged. Holidays here on the islands were about the only time he'd had a chance to take pictures. The day he'd left for the elite boarding school in France where he and Max had been educated, his parents had given him his first camera. He'd loved messing around with it, but too soon his life had filled up with schoolwork and other more active hobbies, like playing polo and rowing. After school, he'd gone on to Oxford and the start of his training as a future leader.

Something occurred to him, and he swallowed against the assault of emotions he couldn't name. "My father was a photographer," he said.

Her brow furrowed and she seemed about to say something, but she bit her lip.

"He's dead," Rik said. He didn't know why, but the thought saddened him. He hadn't wanted to know about the man who fathered him. But suddenly there were things he wished he could ask. Were they anything alike? Had his father felt the same rush behind a camera that he'd just felt? Though snapping pictures of pouting women hardly rated alongside photographing a miracle of nature.

"I'm sorry," she said softly.

He lifted his head. "I'm not. He was a complete stranger."

Her brow furrowed again and for half a second he wondered if she suspected who he was. If she thought he was lying to her. Even though she was the only person in all these months he'd admitted the truth to.

"You have a gift," she said, looking back down at the camera's screen. "You should consider taking up wildlife photography professionally."

Then she looked up at him, and the mischief was back in her eyes. "Let's go home."

Chapter Nine

@LeeHill: @KenzieCole101 Hey Mac, you ok? The radio silence is starting to worry me.

@KenzieCole101: @LeeHill Don't panic. I'm here. Got a little distracted by a mix of vodka, peach schnapps, OJ and cranberry juice.

@LeeHill: @KenzieCole101 You're drinking Sex on the Beach cocktails on the job?

@KenzieCole101: @LeeHill Something like that

Kenzie's phone started to beep the moment the yacht came in sight of Los Pajaros. She sat on the cabin roof, legs swinging over the edge, and scrolled through the day's messages. Two texts from Lee wanting to know why she hadn't been on Twitter all day, another from her mother which she deleted without reading, and a voice message from Neil, several hours old, saying he'd received the pictures and would call as soon as they'd had a chance to discuss them. There hadn't been another call since. Her stomach knotted.

The mobile trilled in her hand, but one glance at the screen and she groaned. She let it ring.

"Aren't you going to answer that?" Rik emerged from the cabin and handed her a chilled glass of the rather superb crisp white wine she'd grown a taste for.

"I'd rather not." But she hit the answer button anyway. Postponing this call would be like trying to stop a volcanic eruption. "Hello, Mum. Look, I can't talk now. I'm expecting a work phone call...yes, I know how late it is...yes, I know normal people don't work these hours." She couldn't keep the exasperation out of her voice.

"I'm sure he's very nice, Mum, but you do know I'm halfway across the planet right now?" Besides, she didn't need fixing up. She was doing rather well on her own in that department.

"I'll call you as soon as I get back, okay?" She disconnected the call and frowned at the screen.

"That sounds like a set-up. Who's the lucky guy?" Rik asked, sitting beside her.

"Shouldn't you be driving this thing?"

He raised an eyebrow and waited. She gave in. "Their accountant. He's steady and dependable, and..." she raised her fingers to make air quotes "...he'll make a really wonderful father."

For that matter, Rik would make a really wonderful father too. She could see him teaching his son to sail, or sitting beside a turtle nest with a little girl in pigtails watching breathlessly as the hatchlings escaped to the sea. He'd be patient and generous and slow to anger. And making babies with him would be so much fun.

She shook her head to clear the vision from her clearly sex-addled brain.

"My mother's convinced being a location scout isn't a real job, and that one day I'm going to stop 'playing' at it and miraculously turn into my brother."

Rik moved back to his post behind the wheel. He stood with a loose gait, legs a little apart, rolling with the pitch of the boat. Masterful, commanding. God, but he was sex on a stick and she wanted to lick him. She crossed her legs.

"What does your brother have that you don't?"

"Aside from the obvious?" Kenzie laughed. "James is the Golden Boy who does everything my parents want. He's taken over the family business, provided them with grandkids, and has the perfect little wife."

She hoped she didn't sound bitter. She liked her sister-in-law, really she did. She was just so tired of always being measured up against Amy and found wanting.

"Me, I'm the screw up. I'm the wrong side of thirty with no man and no baby. And according to my mother I'm doing it all deliberately to hurt her."

It hurt Kenzie far more. Since she'd crossed that decade marker, she'd wanted a baby too. But she wasn't about to marry some dull accountant in order to have one. She wasn't that desperate. Yet.

"So tell your mother you've met someone."

Kenzie shook her head. "Then she'll want to meet him, and that is so not happening." The only man she'd ever taken home was Charlie, and that had been an unmitigated disaster.

"He's not good enough for you," her father had said, more quietly but more emphatically than her mother ever had.

"He's the son of an Earl. How much 'better' do you need him to be?" she'd shot back.

The worst of it was that her parents had been right. Charlie had been very, very bad for her. And the end of their relationship, under the glare of spotlights and video cameras, had been utterly humiliating and utterly devastating. She still hadn't got over it.

She wondered what her parents would make of Rik, scruffy haired, bearded and tattooed. She doubted his having been raised a prince would make any difference to how they'd see him. If he didn't fit into their neat little box, they wouldn't be impressed.

She should know. She'd never fitted those same neat little boxes.

But that was about as far as the resemblance between her and Rik went. She was still an outsider wanting to fit in, while Rik... Beneath the ink and the attitude, Rik was just another Golden Boy.

111

Everything in life had come easily to him. He wore his arrogance and his assurance like a second skin. She'd bet he'd never felt like an outsider. If they'd played footie in Prince Academy, he would have been the star striker.

She sipped the wine. She really needed to check if her local off licence stocked this label. "I've found the 'less is more' approach works best with my parents. I don't tell them anything but the most vanilla details of my life and for the most part they leave me alone."

Rik laughed. "I guess that definitely counts me out of the conversation then. Sex on the beach is definitely more cranberry than vanilla."

"On the beach, on the yacht, up against that palm tree..." She grinned. Being single and child-free definitely had perks.

The mobile vibrated in her hand half a second before it rang. She swung her legs, hopped down from her perch, and answered the call. "Neil?"

Rik adjusted their course and tried to look like he wasn't eaves-dropping while Kenzie paced the deck, her mobile glued to her ear.

"I have meetings set up for Monday morning with the mayor to talk about the tax rebate, then with the harbour master to discuss building the ship, and appointments with a number of hotels to talk preferential rates for the crew." She was a different person on the phone, the cheekiness of a second ago replaced by a brisk, professional tone.

Not for the first time, he wondered how much of who he'd been had been dictated by the job he'd been prepared for all his life. Because being a Prince of Westerwald was so much more than a job description. You didn't turn it off when you clocked out.

While other kids played computer games or watched TV, he and Max had been raised on the tales of their forebears, the laws and legends of their country. Who he was and what he did were woven together, integrated into his DNA. Or so he'd thought.

Without that job, who was he? He wiped a hand over his eyes.

He'd asked the question so many times, and he was still no closer to an answer.

He didn't even have a name he could claim as his own.

Kenzie nodded at whatever Neil said. "I'll meet you at the airport on Monday morning."

She disconnected the call and turned to him, no longer able to suppress her excitement. "I did it! The team will be here on Monday to take over from me."

"You won't be involved in the rest of the film?" Of course, she'd said she'd be leaving in a couple of days. It hadn't sunk in until now that she wouldn't be coming back.

She shook her head. "I'm a scout. I find locations. The production people handle the actual logistical planning of the shoot."

He stared ahead, at the dock that was nothing more than a shadow against the shore. He had just one more day with her. Although this was never meant to be anything more than a way to scratch an itch, a fun way to pass the time; this no longer seemed enough.

"Do you need to work tomorrow, or do film people at least take Sundays off?"

"I can take a day off."

"Good." He held his arm out, and she came to him, snuggling in against his chest. He bent his head to breathe in the fresh summery scent that lingered in her hair. "Then tomorrow you're all mine."

***

He hadn't slept so well in months, and he hadn't even needed a drop of alcohol to fall asleep. And the familiar ache was gone.

Rik slid out of bed and crossed to the glass doors that stood open to the patio. Gauzy white curtains billowed on the breeze.

The sun was a cool pink glow on the eastern horizon, turning the sky pale over the silvery sea. He breathed in the wild ocean scent. Dawn had always been his favourite time of day, that moment's pause before stress and worry and endless meetings replaced the happy anticipation that anything could happen.

Here in the Caribbean, dawn also brought clarity, before the baking sun turned the brain languorous. Every day began with the promise of warmth and sunshine and pleasure, but dawn brought something more: hope.

In his attempt to escape his memories, he'd missed far too many dawns on Los Pajaros.

He stretched and turned back to the room, to the large bed where Kenzie lay, limbs tangled in the sheets, hair splayed out bright and beautiful against the stark white pillows. Soft rosy light crept across the bed, illuminating her.

He was beginning to appreciate that some of the changes wrought in his life were a definite improvement on what he'd had before.

In that grand palace in Neustadt, he'd never once woken with a woman in his bed. By the time he'd been greeted by his valet, with the red leather box filled with schedules, government reports and the morning newspapers, any woman who'd graced his bed had been long gone.

Those moments of stillness at daybreak had been far too brief, and he'd never wanted to share them with anyone. They'd been an indulgence to treasure, since he'd scarcely enjoyed a moment alone.

But with one DNA test everything had turned on its head. He'd had all the alone time he'd ever craved, and more. Yet he'd never felt lonely, not until now, looking at Kenzie asleep in his bed and knowing she might not be there tomorrow.

He wanted to share a lot more dawns with her.

He was over pretending this was just casual sex. What he'd experienced with Kenzie was far more than a random hook-up. He'd begun to feel emotions he'd never believed he would feel, and begun to want things he'd never wanted before.

But before he could take this to another level, first she had to know who he was. Today he would tell her.

He strode back to the bed and slipped beneath the sheets, rolling into the warmth of her body. In Neustadt, he'd also never returned to bed after he'd woken. There'd always been too much to do: agendas to follow, other people's needs to attend to.

Now there was only one item on the agenda: pleasure. His and hers.

He slid a hand over the curve of Kenzie's breast, over the gentle arch of her hip. She sighed, lips parted, caught between sleep and waking.

Stroking back the hair from her neck, he brushed his lips over the sensitive skin at the base of her throat, while his hand slid lower, between her legs. She moaned, and her eyes fluttered open.

"Good morning." He bent to kiss her lips.

She stretched, the movement lazy, sensuous, and smiled. "Good morning."

"There's some place special I'd like to take you today."

She rolled on top of him, her hair tickling his chest. "Does it involve more hiking?"

"No hiking."

"Okay, I'm in." She slid down the length of his body, which hardened instantly at the seductive glide of skin on skin. "But first, I want to swim in the sea."

She slipped from the bed, taking the sheet with her and leaving him aching with unfulfilled desire. It took a few minutes and a lot of deep breathing before he was able to chase after her.

***

@KenzieCole101: I love surprises.

Rik refused to tell her where he was taking her.

The yacht bumped over turbulent waves as they passed the smaller inhabited island of Arelat and approached an island Kenzie couldn't remember visiting before. It was small, not much

115

more than a mountain peak submerged in the sparkling sea, its heavily forested slopes made the island glow like an emerald in the sunlight.

"Which island is this?"

He grinned. "I thought you'd done your homework?"

She screwed up her eyes and tried to picture the aerial maps. Then her eyes widened in shock. "But this is Isla Corona. Isn't this private property? Won't we be trespassing?"

"Yes and yes."

On the sheltered side of the island lay a short marina and a boathouse. There was no-one in sight.

Kenzie shielded her eyes and scanned the landscape. Aside from a gravel road winding away from the marina, there was no other sign of human occupation.

She helped Rik moor the boat beside the dock, practiced enough now to know what to do without instruction, then she followed him down the pier to the rear of the boat house. Under a corrugated iron roof stood a battered open-topped jeep. Rik searched for the key, and found it under the dashboard.

"It looks like an old world war two jeep," she commented.

He jumped into the driver's seat and waved for her to follow. "That's because it is a world war two jeep." He drew in a deep breath, as if psyching himself up for something. "The military gave it to the royal family of Westerwald when they took refuge here during the war."

"So they were lucky enough to escape the war then?" She climbed into the passenger seat.

Rik shook his head. "Not all of them. The Archduke and his son stayed behind. The Archduke was later killed for helping the resistance."

"And his son?"

"He lived." He held her gaze. "He was my grandfather."

She tried to look away, but his dark gaze held her pinned.

"I was born a prince of Westerwald."

116

"I know."

The silence was so complete she could hear the distant chatter of birds.

Rik's face was a mask, giving her no clue how he'd taken her revelation. After a heart-stopping moment in which she prayed for him to say something, anything, he turned the key in the ignition, gunned the motor, and backed the jeep out of its parking.

He neither spoke nor looked at her the entire time they drove along the gravel road which curved along the base of the steep slope and around the island.

Kenzie's heart beat hollowly inside her chest. Was he angry with her? Disappointed? Perhaps she should she have pretended not to know.

She resisted the urge to bury her face in her hands. She wasn't ready to lose him yet. This was supposed to be their special day, not the end of the party. Instead, she gripped the seat, her entire body stiff with tension, and waited for the axe to fall.

The gravel drive twisted through a plantation of tall leatherwood trees, alive with the brightly coloured parrots whose chatter became deafening as the jeep thundered passed. Then the trees fell away and Kenzie gasped.

The gabled house looked like a Hollywood designer's fantasy. The perfect Caribbean colonial mansion: ornate and sprawling, surrounded by elegant colonnaded verandahs, and its white stucco walls were bright in the sun's glare.

Rik stopped the jeep at the bottom of a flight of stairs leading to the main entrance and cut the engine.

"Officially this island belongs to the government, but it has been the royal residence for more than a century."

He still hadn't looked at her.

Kenzie twisted her hands in her lap. "Rik..."

"How long have you known?"

She swallowed hard. "Since the first night we met. I..." oh dear, this wasn't going to sound good. "I read the letter in your pocket

117

and recognised the crest."

He nodded slowly, finally turning to face her. His eyes were shrouded and distant, and her heart sank.

If only he would tell her what he felt... anything to put her out of this dreadful suspense. She almost wished he'd shout and tell her she'd invaded his privacy and betrayed his trust. Anything but this heavy, oppressive silence.

The door at the top of the stairs opened and a woman emerged, coffee-coloured skin, a mop of dark hair turning steely grey, and eyes to match. Her eyes widened as she took them in, then she hurried down the stairs towards them, face breaking into a beaming smile.

Rik climbed out of the jeep. "Hello Marjorie." He wrapped the older woman in a bear hug, and she squeezed him back tightly. She looked as if she was about to cry.

Kenzie sat unmoving in the jeep, feeling very much like an intruder. An outsider. Unwanted. It was a feeling she'd had her whole life, one she hadn't experienced since the day she'd met Rik, but now it was back in spades, and worse than ever.

"Where have you been? You've had us all worried sick!" Marjorie said. "There's a pile of letters and messages from your family waiting inside, in case you ever showed up."

"I've been staying at Adam's villa."

The woman's eyes widened in horror. "You've been right here in the islands and you didn't come to see me?"

Kenzie wouldn't have believed it if she hadn't seen it with her own eyes. Rik blushed like a naughty schoolboy caught in a prank.

With a look bordering on desperation, he turned to her. "Marjorie, I'd like you to meet Kenzie."

But he still wouldn't make eye contact.

Well, at least it was better than a slap in the face. Putting on her professional smile, though her legs felt like rubber, Kenzie climbed out of the jeep. "It's a pleasure to meet you."

She held out her hand for a shake, but instead, Marjorie hugged her. Caught off guard, Kenzie could do nothing but hug her back. The older woman smelled of cinnamon and sugar, like every birthday and Christmas rolled into one.

"So are you the reason Rik's been keeping a low profile?"

Kenzie was sure she blushed as vivid as Rik had. "We only met a few days ago."

Marjorie sent Rik a searching look. Then she looped her arm through Kenzie's and led her up the stairs towards the house. Rik trailed behind.

Kenzie had never seen a house as beautiful as this. Charlie's ancestral pile of grey cold stone paled into insignificance beside this house. The entrance was a grand double volume space, warm and full of light, with a double marble staircase rising up to a gallery above.

For an instant, Kenzie pictured a Christmas tree there, in the space between the two flights of arcing stairs. She blinked and the image disappeared.

Marjorie led them across the hall and through a set of French doors onto another verandah. The gardens dropped in terraces of green lawns and bright-coloured flowerbeds to a rocky beach far below.

"Make yourself comfortable, and I'll fetch some tea." Marjorie patted Kenzie's arm and let her go. Kenzie had an overwhelming urge to cling to the older woman for safety. She dragged in a steadying breath instead.

"You need a shave, young man," Marjorie said as she passed Rik in the doorway.

Kenzie turned away to look out over the gardens. She tensed as Rik came to stand beside her. He leaned a hip against the stone balustrade and crossed his arms over his chest.

"So are you a gold digger or did you just fancy sex with a royal?"

The red haze descended. "Neither." Kenzie didn't get angry often, but when she did it was impossible to stem the flood. She rounded on him. "I didn't want this! All I wanted was an introduction to the mayor. I most certainly didn't want complications. You kissed *me* remember?"

He frowned. Either he didn't like being called a complication, or he didn't like the idea that she wasn't as keen as he was. Either way, tough. He could lump it if he didn't like it.

She leaned in, struggling to keep her voice low. "You're the one who brought me here. I could quite happily have gone on pretending you were just another bad boy out for a good time."

But now the truth was out there, and it changed everything. He wasn't a pirate, and he was nothing like the bad boys she'd dated before, and the biggest truth, the one she really didn't want to face, was that this was a man she could lose her heart to. Prince and all.

"So you're not going to sell your story to the press? '*How I bagged a prince!*'"

She jumped back as if she'd been burnt. How dare he! How dare he think she'd stoop so low? Her voice shook. "Not everything is about you."

She wanted to hurt him as much as he'd hurt her with his mistrust and his presumption. "You *used* to be a prince. But now you're nothing. No, you're less than nothing, because you're not even a productive member of society. You drift through life taking what you want and thinking of no-one but yourself."

Perhaps it wasn't Rik she was talking about any longer, but her words achieved their mark. He flinched away from her as if she'd struck him.

"And *I'm* not for the taking, Rik!"

His eyes glittered. "Now there you're wrong." He stepped closer, boxing her in against the balustrade. "You've been mine for the taking from the moment I met you, and I'll prove it."

His hands were in her hair, his mouth crushed down on hers. She wanted so badly to fight him off. She wanted to put her hands on his chest and shove him away.

Her hands made it as far as his chest. And there they stayed.

How could she fight him off when her own body gave in and

120

betrayed her at the first touch of his lips on hers? When her knees melted and her very core turned to liquid heat.

She pressed against him and felt the answering hardness in him. His arm wrapped around her, pulling her tighter against him as he deepened the kiss, punishing her, persuading her.

When they finally broke apart, breathing heavily, neither moved.

"I'm sorry," he whispered. "I'm a jerk."

"Yes. You are." She struggled to breathe. "And I'm sorry I said you are nothing. That was cruel and inexcusable."

His grip on her tightened. "But true. I've spent these last few months wallowing and feeling sorry for myself. It's time I snap out of it and stop thinking only of myself."

Their gazes snagged, held. The ground suddenly seemed unsteady beneath her feet. Lord help her, but she was in trouble.

"I would never, ever go to the media," she said fervently, needing him to believe it.

He stroked her fringe away from her face, tucking it behind her ear. "I should have told you who I was right from the beginning. I wasn't honest with you, but I want to be."

She shook her head. On this they would have to agree to disagree. He should never have told her who he really was.

At the sound of the clatter of teacups, they leapt apart. Rik hurried to take the silver tray from Marjorie's hands, then they sat at a wooden table on the verandah and Marjorie poured the tea.

The older woman glanced between them, and Kenzie felt her face heat up again. She could only imagine how wanton she must seem, with her hair mussed and her lips bruised by Rik's kiss. It took all her effort to play at being civilised and make polite conversation while her blood thrummed in her veins and her body screamed for Rik's hands back on her skin.

They sipped tea and ate cinnamon buns fresh from the oven, while Rik and Marjorie caught up with news of people they both knew. Marjorie had been his nanny, Kenzie discovered, though when her charges had left for boarding school she'd returned to her homeland and taken this position as housekeeper.

"Your mother calls every week," Marjorie said.

Rik stiffened. Kenzie was learning to recognise that look – it meant he didn't want to talk about it.

Either Marjorie hadn't recognised it, or she didn't care. She bulldozed on. "She misses you and wants to talk to you. Call her."

Rik shook his head, subtly but unmistakeably.

"She'll be at Max's engagement party. You'll be able to talk to her then."

"I won't be there."

That was news to Kenzie. She scrutinised his expression, but he was doing his impression of a mask again.

She shouldn't get involved. She didn't want to get involved. But it also didn't take a genius to know that the brooding look Rik wore so much of the time covered a deep hurt. She'd known from that first night they'd met that something was broken inside him.

Her chest pulled tight.

She'd tried before to fix the people she loved and every time she was the one who ended up hurt. She couldn't fix Rik. But there was one thing she could do for him.

She set her teacup down. "What are the chances I can get a guided tour?"

Rik cast her a grateful smile and rose to hold her chair for her as she stood. Ever the gentleman. "Will you excuse us, Marjorie?"

The older woman smiled indulgently. "I'll have lunch ready right here at one."

Rik took Kenzie's hand to lead her back into the house, but as she passed Marjorie, the older woman laid a hand on her arm. Her voice was low enough that Rik wouldn't hear: "Rik doesn't bring a girl home after just a few days."

@KenzieCole101: Scrap that. I think I hate surprises.

Chapter Ten

Kenzie didn't really want a guided tour, she'd only suggested it so he could escape the kind of inquisition she was all too familiar with, but she got one anyway. Rik traipsed her through formal reception rooms and dining rooms able to seat dozens, the high ceilinged library, the ballroom...

Why anyone would need a ballroom on a remote and otherwise unoccupied tropical island was anyone's guess, but the space quite literally took her breath away. Even with the shutters closed, streaks of golden light fell in patterns across the gleaming parquet floor.

Beneath a curved high ceiling, the room was graceful and elegant. A room made for dancing. Closing her eyes, she imagined a band at the furthest end of the room, a jazz band, white suited, dark-skinned, the deep steady bass sweeping the dancers around the room.

The place must be a bitch to dust, though. She was glad she didn't have to do it.

"This place shouldn't be left standing empty. This is a house for parties and..." She blinked as the thought blinded her. "And film shoots." She turned to Rik. "There are so many amazing locations around these islands. All it needs is someone with vision, someone who could facilitate the shoots and make sure that film companies have what they need, and this could become a real hot spot."

She almost trembled with excitement, every neuron in her brain firing on all cylinders. This was a job she could do. It felt like the job she was born to do. She had the vision, she knew what film companies would need, she could stay...

She blinked and shook her head. She was also a woman, and a woman with no Caribbean connections.

"The palace at Neustadt is much more impressive," Rik said. "The tour guides call it Baroque, but really it's more Rococo in style." He faced her. "I'm sorry. I must be boring you."

"Not at all. An amateur interest in architecture is what got me into this job in the first place."

Lee had been up all night, working on a set design for a period television show. After Kenzie had made the dozenth cup of coffee, she'd glanced over Lee's drawings and picked them to shreds. It was after she'd brought out her photo albums to prove a point that Lee suggested she make a career change. Photographing locations sure beat every other job she'd ever had.

Rik led her upstairs, to the private apartments. High-ceilinged, full of sunlight and space. What a place for kids to grow up. She shut down that thought. It must be the heat...that made it twice in two days she'd thought of Rik and kids in the same breath.

Not going to happen. Remember the last time she'd contemplated starting a family with someone?

Rik opened the door on a bedroom the same size as the entire Shoreditch flat she and Lee shared.

"Oh wow, look at that bed!" She took a running dive for the four poster and landed in a giggly heap right in the centre. It was just as lusciously comfortable as it looked. She lay on her back and stared up at the ceiling where a rattan fan churned, setting the diaphanous white curtains of the four-poster dancing.

Rik climbed on the bed beside her, lying mere millimetres away as he also stared up at the ceiling. "I always liked it here. Some of the best moments in my life were spent right here in the islands. No press, no schedules, just our family together."

"And now you get to stay permanently."

"I'm not here permanently. I'm just passing through, until I figure out who I am and what to do with the rest of my life."

She propped herself up on an elbow to look at him. "You're wallowing again. It's time you get over yourself. You're the same person you always were. None of us are the sum total of our job descriptions."

"Being the hereditary ruler of Westerwald was more than a job description. Without that title, I don't even have a name."

She sat up, angry with him again. "We're also more than an accident of our births. Do you even know how lucky you are? You get to start over with a fresh slate. You can re-invent yourself. You can be anyone you want to be."

That feeling she'd had on the yacht, the night they'd sailed back from dinner at Christianstad, washed over her. In that moment she'd felt like a new person, a better person.

And she was. She'd left the past behind. Her career was opening up before her, full of promise. If she could do it, then Rik could too.

"There's always a Plan B," she said. "And usually it's better than Plan A ever was."

"My mother said something like that the last time we spoke, the night she told me she'd known all along I wasn't my father's child." He stared up at the ceiling. "I'm sure you've heard the story."

"I read an article or two, but I don't really follow the gossip columns."

"In Westerwald it was front page news." He jumped off the bed and began to pace the room, scowling, shoulders hunched, the ultimate brooding bad boy. This was the Rik she'd met in the bar that first night. Moody, dangerous, and sexy as hell. Her heart thumped a discordant rhythm.

"My mother was pregnant when she married my father. At least the man I believed was my father. She knew she was pregnant with another man's bastard and she married him anyway. Then she passed me off as his child. She had to know that one day the truth would out. She knew it would come back to bite us, to bite me, but selfishly she did it anyway. I'm just grateful my father never lived to know the truth. That he never found out how she lied to him his entire life."

"Perhaps she did it for you. To give her unborn baby a chance at a better life and the kind of father he deserved."

He snorted.

But then what would he know about how far a mother would go for her baby?

Rik stopped pacing and thrust his hands into his pockets. "Do you know what the worst is? It's the stuff that didn't make the papers. I was conceived in a darkened corner of Studio 54, and my mother was drunk at the time. At least that was her excuse for her lapse in judgment. That's what she called it...called me...a lapse in judgment."

And there it was, the hurt plain to see.

He wasn't a bad boy. He never had been. He was a complicated, careful man who buried his hurt deep. And that was so much worse, because that made him a man she could truly fall in love with. A man she wanted to heal.

She resisted the urge to reach out and comfort him.

Who was she kidding? She'd learned a long time ago you couldn't heal someone else's heartbreak.

"And your biological father – do you know anything about him?"

Rik shrugged. "My mother told me his name. Robert Ellis... he was some sort of fashion photographer. Fashion! Of all the meaningless professions in the world."

She forced herself to breathe deeply, to make her tone light. "Yeah, films are pretty meaningless too, but we all have to make a living somehow, you know. Or maybe you don't. We don't all have trust funds to finance our lifestyles."

He straightened his shoulders, indignant. "I told you when we met that I'm not some spoilt rich kid living it up on inherited money. I was raised to make a difference in the world."

"So make a difference in the world. You have money, you have influence, use both. You could do anything you wanted. You could climb Everest or run charities for orphans, or become a spokesperson for the sea turtles. You're a celebrity, so use it."

She'd never thought she'd be giving anyone advice to court the press, but since she wasn't going to be around when it happened, she felt safe. Do as I say, not as I do.

"What if this is what you were meant to do?" she continued. "You have contacts and skills that could be useful to the islands. The Los Pajaros archipelago is the poor cousin to the rest of the Caribbean, virtually closed to the outside world. With good marketing and someone to manage it, it could become as popular and as profitable as the better known island groups."

He smiled and his shoulders relaxed. "You make a good argument."

She was grateful for that smile, grateful that the brooding darkness had been averted. She rose from the bed. This was all too heavy for an island fling. Too many memories stirred beneath the surface. She needed to get away.

"Everything always works out in the end." She headed for the door. She prayed it was true.

***

They crossed the vast space of the entrance hall, heading back to the terrace.

"Back in the sixties my grandparents often had parties here," Rik said. "And their Christmas party for the under-privileged children of the islands is the stuff of legend." He sighed and stuck his hands in the pockets of his chinos. "Life was simpler then. By the time we came along, there wasn't time for parties. Life just got too busy, my father always said. He taught us to sail, but he spent as much time locked away in his office as he did with us."

She tried to imagine growing up as the child of a head of state, and failed dismally. The family bakery, though it had been in the Cole family for four generations, and large as it had grown, paled into insignificance beside Rik's family business.

"It must have been hard on you, growing up like that."

He shook his head. "It's strange, but I don't think my father really liked it here. Back home in Westerwald he was very different. He always made time for us. We were very close. He taught me to sail, and to play polo." He swallowed. "We were so much alike. Everyone said so. I still can't believe I'm not his son."

"He was your father for thirty five years in every way that matters. So what if he wasn't your biological father?"

"Blood is the only thing that matters."

"Bullshit."

When they reached the terrace, Marjorie was laying out a table for lunch beneath a trellis of magenta bougainvillea. Roast beef with all the trimmings, followed by fresh strawberries and cream. And rum punch.

How she'd managed such a feast for unexpected guests, Kenzie had no idea. If she and Lee had unexpected guests the best they could hope for was peanut butter sandwiches or Coco Pops.

She looked at the two place settings on the table. "Aren't you joining us?"

"Not today." The older woman's expression held amusement. "It doesn't take a mind reader to know you two want to be alone. But maybe next time you come back..."

Kenzie looked away. There wasn't going to be a next time. The countdown was already on. In twenty-four hours she'd be on a plane and leaving Los Pajaros, probably forever.

She didn't know why that thought made her want to cry. A few days ago she'd hated everything about this place.

Marjorie left them alone, and they ate, making nothing but small talk, the heaviness of their earlier conversation banished.

Good, because she didn't want to waste her last hours here in talk.

As they ate, their gazes lingered, their fingers brushed, setting her body humming again, like one of those wires that crossed vast expanses of wilderness. If the wire pulled any tauter, it would snap, and the spark would set fire to everything it touched.

She took her glass of rum punch and moved to lean on the balustrade overlooking the neat croquet lawn at the side of the house. She closed her eyes and breathed in the scent of freshly cut grass. In her mind's eye she could see the lawn, golden in the afternoon light, filled with men in dinner jackets and women in big hats milling around as waist-coated waiters walked between them with silver trays of champagne.

She opened her eyes, banishing the vision. "This place must take an army of people to keep it maintained. Where is everyone?"

Rik moved to stand beside her. "Most of the staff go to Arelat on Sundays, to church and to spend the day with their families." He removed the glass of punch from her fingers and set it aside. "We're as good as alone here."

She straightened, her stomach doing little leaps. Now *this* was what their fling was all about...not talk, but action. "And there's that magnificent big bed upstairs..."

"Who needs a bed?" He lifted her off her feet and sat her down on the sun-warmed balustrade, moving between her legs. His fingers slid over her crotch, teasing her through her jeans. She squirmed.

His eyes were so dark they were black holes, sucking her in.

"Not here, Rik. What if Marjorie were to come back out?"

He grinned. "Let's hope she doesn't."

She moaned in pleasure, unable to hold back the sound or the impending climax. Just like that, she was so tantalising close she wanted to scream. She bit down on her lip, drawing blood, as the waves swept through her and she fell limp against his shoulder.

"You are a very bad man, Prince Fredrik."

He laughed. "Just Rik. And don't tell me you don't love it."

***

@KenzieCole101: In most fairy tales the bad boy turns into a prince. Just once I'd like to kiss a prince and have him turn into a steady dependable boy.

After lunch they said their goodbyes to Marjorie, promising to visit again, and Rik sailed them back to Los Pajaros, to his friend's ultra-modern villa overlooking the sea like a god looking down from Olympus. No tin-roofed shack for the exiled prince. If this was just the guest villa, then Kenzie couldn't imagine what the main house looked like.

He secured the yacht in the villa's boathouse, then they walked hand-in-hand up the stairs hewn out of the rock face.

There were more stairs than she could count and the only way she'd made it up them last night was because Rik had promised her a bed at the end of it. The bed, and everything in it, had been worth the climb.

Halfway up, the stairs branched. Instead of leading her up to the villa this time, Rik led her down to a private beach, a narrow strip of dark sand, still wet from the outgoing tide and hemmed in by large boulders. They undressed and ran into the sea, laughing and splashing each other like children released from a day of school.

Kenzie had never swum naked in the sea before. Warm water caressed her bare skin, teasing unfamiliar places. She stood with her legs apart, enjoying the sensuous way the waves pummelled at her. She lifted her face to the sun's kiss, past caring what it did to her skin, loving its sensual touch.

Rik moved to stand behind her, pressing against her bare bottom. His hands stroked over her breasts which were heavy and ached with need. She laid her head back on his shoulder as her limbs turned liquid.

He bent his head to kiss her, and he tasted of rum and coconut and sea salt. Her stomach tightened. He feathered kisses down her neck and along her collarbone, and she turned into him, wrapping her hands around the stunning strength of his erection.

He removed her hands. "If you keep that up, I might not be accountable for my actions. And sea water and sand are not conducive to what I'd want to do to you."

"We managed yesterday."

"I was desperate yesterday."

"And you're not desperate now?" She rubbed herself against him.

He growled low in his throat. "Don't play with fire unless you want to get burned."

She grinned. "Oh, I want to get burned." She slipped away, splashing through the waves, glancing back over her shoulder to make sure he followed.

He caught her up in the shallows, grabbing her from behind as she squealed and tried to wriggle away, but he held her fast, picking her up and carrying her out of the water to the enormous rocks that sheltered the little cove.

He deposited her on her hands and knees on a rock. She tried to face him, but he held her still. "Don't move," he commanded, laying a firm hand on her back.

She didn't.

The sun dried her skin, and the light sea breeze stung a pleasurable awareness to her exposed parts as he moved away to search through the clothes they'd strewn on the beach. She heard the familiar rip of foil and her stomach muscles clenched in anticipation. Then he was behind her, his hands on her hips.

She gasped as he entered her, gasped again as he pulled out and the breeze caressed her in his place. She arched her back, bracing herself against the hard rock as he set a steady rhythm and she gave herself over to the sensation, closing her eyes so that every sense was focussed on this moment, on this joining of two bodies, on the intense waves of pleasure roiling through her.

Her orgasm ripped through her, purifying as fire. She felt like a new person indeed. It was impossible to remember past mistakes when in the grip of making a beautiful new one.

***

As the sunlight faded, they climbed the stairs to the villa and sat on a swing chair on the frangipani-scented patio, limbs entwined, to watch the sun set across the sea. Behind the villa, the hills turned a red-gold in the dying light, and lights began to flicker on in the shacks hidden between the trees in the valley beyond. From the distance, the soft, compelling sound of a steel band drifted up to them on the breeze.

Darkness swallowed them, but neither wanted to break this moment to get up and switch on the lights. So they rocked gently, and watched the moonlight falling on the beach far below, and held each other.

The music of the steel drums faded into the darkness leaving only the sound of the ocean, the song of night insects, and the distant call of a bat. The waves moved in on the offensive, then retreated, much like her and Rik, an endless backwards and forwards, in and out like the tide, neither gaining ground. Making no progress. Going nowhere.

High up in the cloudless sky a shooting star shot across the heavens. She closed her eyes to make a wish.

"What is it you want, Mackenzie Cole?" Rik asked.

She wanted the same as every woman. She wanted more than a temporary island romance. She wanted a man who'd stick by her side no matter what. And she wanted a home and a family and respect.

She opened her eyes. "If you were on Twitter, you'd know that already."

Chapter Eleven

When Kenzie woke, the first thing she saw was the sky. Not the crystal clear, cerulean sky she'd grown accustomed to, but a heavy sky the colour of charcoal, filled with roiling crowds.

Rik had predicted a storm. How fitting that it should cast a pall over her final day.

She rolled against him and cuddled into his side. She could practically hear the distant wall clock ticking out the seconds, counting down the time she had left with him.

Counting down the time she had left on Los Pajaros. Who would have thought, mere days ago when she'd hit nothing but road block after road block, that she'd fall in love with the place?

Or with a man she'd only just met.

She slipped from the bed and padded through to the kitchen to switch the coffee machine on. By the time Rik joined her, wearing nothing but drawstring jogging bottoms low on his hips, she had breakfast and fresh coffee ready.

Though the air had turned chilly, making it too cool to eat outside on the patio, she still opened all the doors, and the sweet, heavy scent of frangipani blossoms wafted in, mingling with the bitter coffee aroma. But all she could taste in her mouth was bitterness.

"I have to go." She broke apart the flaky croissant with her fingers. "I need to pick the team up at the airport and then we have meetings scheduled with the mayor and the harbour master."

"What happens when your meetings are over?"

"I fly back to London."

He steepled his fingers and leaned back in his chair, and for a moment she caught a glimpse of the kind of ruler he would have been: serious, focussed, and just a little intimidating.

"So your work on this particular project is done and you're back to unemployment?"

She frowned. "You sound like my mother."

"Stay with me."

"What?"

"If you don't have any reason to hurry back to London, stay here in Los Pajaros for a few more days. A week, perhaps."

"My flight's already booked."

Rik leaned forward. "I'll book you another."

"I have to check out of the resort and return my rental car this morning."

"You won't need either of them."

She kept her eyes down. Staying here in Los Pajaros would mean loads more phenomenal sex. Her body was already saying 'yes please!' to that. But staying would also mean she could no longer pretend this was a simple one-night stand. Staying would mean getting *involved*. Or at least more involved than she already was.

"Let me just get through this meeting, okay?"

"You'll think about it?"

"I'll think about it." How to stop thinking about it enough to concentrate in the meeting was going to be more of an issue.

He rose. "I'll drive you back to the resort so you can check out and fetch your rental. After your meeting at the harbour master's we can meet at the end of Pier Four, and you can tell me your decision."

She nodded.

The drive to the resort flashed by too quickly. Kenzie stared out the window, absorbing every sight and sound, every memory, every moment. The car jolted through ruts and deep, stagnant puddles, past wooden shacks behind low slatted fences where dark-eyed children grinned and waved as they drove past. They passed a lone store, tiny and thatch-roofed with the ubiquitous Coca-Cola sign hanging from the eaves, faded by the sun.

She didn't want to leave. She wanted to explore every corner of these islands, wanted to drink cocktails beneath the setting sun and swim in the ocean again, and hear the monkeys chatter in the trees on Tortuga.

But if she stayed...

Rik wouldn't understand. He'd never been in love. How convenient was that? If he'd never been in love, then he'd never been hurt. He didn't know how the end of a relationship could tear you apart. And with a man like Rik the end would be inevitable.

He'd only asked her to stay for a week at most.

He pulled up beneath the portico at the hotel entrance. "I'll see you at one." He leaned across and tucked a fresh frangipani flower behind her ear.

She nodded, unable to speak, and stepped out of the car. Without a backward glance she hurried inside to pack her bags.

***

It was hard to concentrate. Voices droned on around her and the air felt heavy. Kenzie swigged from her coffee cup and forced her focus back into the boardroom where the production designer and the ship's master craftsman debated the finer points of pirate ship design. She stifled a yawn.

She hadn't had her full eight hours last night, but then it had also been her last night with Rik. She hadn't wanted to miss a moment.

Perhaps it didn't have to be the end...

The harbour master's boardroom was surprisingly modern,

with trendy furnishings and damask wallpaper patterned in black and white. The wide first floor windows looked out into the leafy trees beyond, their colour vivid against the overcast sky.

In the muggy tropical heat, her production team were sweating in spite of their short sleeves. After the chill of autumnal London this closeness must be a massive shock.

Thunder rolled, deep and ominous, in the distance.

When the meeting finally adjourned, Kenzie stuffed her notebook and pen into her rucksack. It was already one o'clock and Rik would be waiting for her at Pier Four. She needed to see him with a desperation that bordered on pain, a physical itch so intense it needed the emotional equivalent of calamine lotion.

"Well done, Kenzie." Neil shuffled his papers together, not looking up. "I'll call the other scouts off and let them know we'll be shooting the entire Caribbean section of the film here."

Her heart thumped loudly against her ribs. She'd done it!

He looked up from his papers. "Do you have any plans for the next week?"

Stay on Los Pajaros to indulge in more hot sex? She shook her head. "No. No plans."

"Great. We've had scouts out searching for a baroque palace for the European scenes, and they've not had much luck. Can you believe one actually brought me pictures of Blenheim? Like I hadn't thought of that!" He tucked his file under his arm. "You want to have a crack at it?"

Would she ever? She looked toward the window where raindrops had begun to spatter against the glass. Rik would get very wet if she kept him waiting much longer.

"Can I get back to you?"

"Sure. Just let my coordinator know and she'll make your new travel arrangements. Have a safe flight."

Kenzie grabbed her rucksack and headed for the door.

She left her bags in the rental and ran all the way to Pier Four. Great big raindrops smacked down, far more dramatic than the fine, misting European rain she was used to.

By the time she reached the Pier, chest burning and her hair plastered to her face, the rain mingled with her hot, salty tears.

Rik waited at the end of the pier, his back to her as he leaned on the steel railing, looking out over the harbour, oblivious to the rain. She stopped a few paces away from him and he turned.

She managed a smile. "Mission accomplished!"

He grinned. "So you'll stay?"

"Neil has offered me a chance to scout the European leg of the shoot too."

She barely caught the look of incredulity in his eyes before the mask slipped into place.

"I'm not looking for a relationship, Rik." Not with *you*. "You knew that."

"Neither am I. I just don't want the fun to end yet."

Typical bloody Golden Boy. Making this all about what *he* wanted – a quick fling, a little fun. What about what she needed?

She shook her head. "If I stay, this won't be a one-night stand any more, and neither of us is ready for anything more." She swallowed. "Are we?"

"Don't go." He made it sound like a command and her back bristled. She wasn't his plaything, to keep for as long as it amused him. And he hadn't answered her question. Which was an answer in itself.

Pain gnawed at her chest. "It's like the forest, another rainy season and you won't even remember I was here."

Whereas she would never forget.

Another moment with him and she wouldn't have the strength to walk away.

"Goodbye, Rik."

She managed to put one foot in front of another and keep going without looking back, though her feet dragged like lead. By the time she reached the rental car her eyes were aching and swollen from the tears streaming down her face.

She sat behind the wheel for a long moment before she pulled the frangipani blossom from her hair. It lay limp and wilted in her palm. Like their fling, its time was over.

@KenzieCole101: @ProducerNeil I'd like to take you up on that offer. I'm thinking Poland for baroque palaces.

Chapter Twelve

Rik swam through the churning grey water. The shore seemed no closer than it had ten minutes ago, though his arms ached with the effort. Every morning since he'd arrived in Los Pajaros he'd pushed himself this way, to the very edge of collapse.

Every morning he felt that temptation to give in, to let the water drag him away. But he kept on fighting. It was a triumph of sorts, knowing that for another day he'd beaten not only the sea but his own demons.

So why hadn't he done the same with Kenzie? Why hadn't he chased after her and fought for her?

He was used to getting what he wanted. Even here on the islands. He wanted anonymity, he got it. He wanted a favour, he called the mayor. He wanted sex, he found someone.

So now that he wanted more than sex, when he wanted to give these new feelings he was experiencing a shot, why hadn't he stopped Kenzie from getting on that plane?

Because of the fear in her eyes. She'd been scared and he hadn't known how to deal with it. He had no idea what she was scared of, or how to fix it.

His arms pulled against the tide, tiring now. He fought harder, pouring all his frustration into beating the unbeatable.

What could he do to make Kenzie want him? He was a

gentleman. He wouldn't hurt her. They could have so much fun together. And the sex...

He could still feel her on his skin, the slide of her hair, the softness of her body pressed against him.

His feet found purchase on the gravelly floor and he rose, wading out of the sea.

Perhaps the problem was that he didn't really have a clue how to seduce a woman. Back when he'd been a prince, it had been so easy. He'd determined his target, made a few calls, had his intelligence people research her until he knew her weakness, and then he'd honed in. Most women were easy. They wanted money or fame or appreciation. Some just wanted sex.

But with Kenzie, he had no idea what she wanted. He wasn't even sure if she knew what she wanted. She'd been hurt before; she'd said as much. But even this career she chased after wasn't her main driving force. If it were, she'd have taken it more seriously. She'd have had a five year plan, at least.

He frowned as he scrubbed himself dry with the towel.

Though the storm had blown itself out through the night, the air was still chilly and damp. He looked up at the foreboding sky.

He'd followed his instincts with Kenzie and so far his instincts hadn't been wrong. This wasn't the end.

All he needed to know was what Kenzie wanted, and how he could make it happen.

Since he no longer had a secret service at his fingertips to do the research for him, he'd have to do it himself.

***

@KenzieCole101: I'm re-packing my bags tonight. Out with the suntan lotion and in with the winter coat.

Rik pressed the door buzzer and leaned against the wall. The sound of a TV within the flat sounded loud through the plain white door. Rugby commentary? He hadn't taken Kenzie for a rugby fan.

The chain rattled behind the door and a latch slid open. The door opened a fraction before it was flung wide.

Rik's eyes opened wide at the bare-chested young man who'd opened the door. He looked like a GQ model; tall, with fair curly hair, bright blue eyes, and dimples that deepened as he gave Rik the once over. And had Rik mentioned? … He was shirtless.

Scratch GQ model. He looked more like a male stripper.

"Who the hell are you?" Rik demanded.

"I'm Lee, and who the hell are you? Or more importantly, what can I do for you?"

This was *Lee*? Kenzie's best friend and flatmate was a *man*? Rik's hands fisted. Best friends, or friends with benefits? He was tempted to turn around and leave.

He took a deep breath and forced himself to smile. This time he wasn't going to give up without a fight.

"Is Kenzie home?" He only just managed to keep his voice on the polite side of a snarl.

"Mac, it's for you." Lee called over his shoulder into the flat. With the grace of a dancer, he turned and headed towards the sofa in front of the TV, where he stretched out his long, lean limbs. Not only was he shirtless, but he was barefoot too. He was dressed in nothing but low-slung jeans that revealed way too much honed torso, in Rik's opinion.

"Who is it?" Kenzie's voice drifted down the corridor from an inner room.

"No idea. Didn't introduce himself. But he's *hot*." Lee called back. Then to Rik: "Make yourself at home."

Rik settled into the one available armchair and spared a glance for the TV before looking back at Lee, who eyed him with cheerful amusement.

"I'm Rik," he said, more to pass the time than to make polite conversation.

Lee's eyes rounded and he sat upright, slinging his bare feet off the sofa. "You don't look much like a pirate."

Rik didn't have a chance to puzzle out that cryptic comment, since Kenzie chose that moment to make her entrance. He rose.

Dressed in a wide-necked white tee over a lacy camisole top and a pair of denim cut-offs, her only concession to the chill of autumnal London was a pair of black tights.

He swallowed. The tights emphasised the shapely length of her legs, and as for that slip of black lace dipping over the curves of her breasts...

He lifted his gaze to her face.

"You clean up nicely," she observed, eyeing his clean-shaven face and the tailored suit. Her face was expressionless but her eyes looked like they'd been bruised.

"And you look awful."

"Lack of sleep does that to her." Lee said cheerfully. Two sets of glaring eyes turned to him and he held up his hands in a gesture of retreat.

"I've had a stomach bug. I didn't expect to see you here." *Or ever*, her tone implied.

He hadn't exactly expected a warm welcome, but this was verging on hostile. "Can we talk?"

"Sure." She glanced at her flatmate. "Isn't there somewhere else you could be right now?"

Lee grinned, cheeks dimpling. "And miss all the fun? No way!" Kenzie frowned and he sighed. "Alright, then. I suppose I could watch the rest of the game down at the pub."

"Thanks."

Lee gave her a peck on the cheek as he passed her on his way to the door, whispering loud enough for his voice to carry to Rik, "Don't do anything I wouldn't do."

Kenzie cuffed his arm. "That doesn't leave much, does it?"

The door closed behind Lee, and they were alone.

She crossed to the sofa Lee had just vacated and sat with her legs curled beneath her. "This is an unexpected pleasure."

Rik resumed his seat on the armchair. "You never told me Lee was a man."

"Didn't I? He's no threat to your ego, you know. He bats for the other side."

His brow knotted.

She smiled, but it didn't reach her eyes. "You really have lived a sheltered life. Lee's gay."

Ah.

"Not to put too fine a point on it, but what are you doing here?"

"I need a date for an event, and I was hoping you were free."

"What's the event in aid of?"

"You read the letter."

Her face froze. Slowly, she shook her head. "I thought you weren't going."

"I changed my mind."

She crossed her arms over her chest. "Why? And why me? I'm not an A-list party kind of girl. I'm sure you won't have any trouble finding someone who enjoys being a rich man's arm candy."

"Marjorie couldn't make it so I need a back up plan. You seem to be pretty good at those. Besides, it's not an A-list party. It's friends and family only."

He wasn't above playing on that soft heart of hers. He leaned forward, elbows on his knees. "My mother's going to be there. I need moral support. I need you."

"Where and when is this party?"

"Tonight in Neustadt."

"Tonight?" She shook her head. "I can't. I'm busy. I'm flying to Warsaw in the morning."

"I know. You're scouting for a Baroque palace."

She uncrossed her arms. "How on earth do you know that?"

"Little thing called Twitter. I'm learning how to use it. Don't forget your camera, because you're going to be inside a palace in Neustadt that's never been seen before. If it doesn't work for you, I'll put you on a plane to Warsaw myself."

Her eyes opened wide as saucers, her excitement clear. "You'll get me permission to shoot *inside* the palace in Neustadt?"

"I know the owner." The corner of her mouth lifted and her eyes sparkled. It was a much better look on her than the reticent, thin-lipped expression that had greeted him. "I have an appointment at Nieborow Palace tomorrow."

"Cancel it. Or better yet, I'll call the Minister and cancel for you. We served together on a committee for European heritage a couple of years ago."

"That won't be necessary."

She licked her lips, and he smiled. Though he knew it was the thought of photographing the holy grail of film locations, a real live royal palace, that was piquing her interest rather than seeing him again, he'd take what he could get.

"You know I don't even own a dress."

He grinned. "That cocktail dress you wore to dinner in Christianstad will be perfect."

***

Her bag was already packed. All she had to do was add in the dress, a pair of killer heels – the only ones she possessed – and a make-up bag. At the last minute she threw in the earrings she'd inherited from her grandmother.

"Will we have time to get dressed before the party?" It was already growing dark in London and Westerwald was an hour ahead.

"We can change on the plane," Rik said, leaning against the doorframe and watching her. She wished she'd bothered to at least make the bed. Or hide the bin of used tissues she'd filled crying herself to sleep last night.

Tonight there'd be no need for the tissues. Tonight she'd be back in his arms.

She snapped her suitcase shut and zipped it closed. "I'll need to change into something more appropriate to travel in, then we can go."

His gaze raked down her stockinged legs and he smiled. "You're perfect as you are. But you'll need a coat. It's cold and wet outside."

She hadn't noticed, since she'd spent practically the entire day in bed. But when was England anything but cold and wet? She'd scarcely been gone a day and a half and already she felt homesick for the Caribbean.

Slipping on her boots, she grabbed her phone and charger, and left Rik to follow with her suitcase. She stuck a scribbled post-it note on the television for Lee, collected her coat and camera bag, and let them out of the flat.

A car waited at the kerb, revving to life as they emerged from the building. No, not a car. A luxury sedan with tinted windows.

Rik stowed her luggage in the boot and opened the door for her to slide inside. She settled back against the leather, feeling woefully under-dressed for the setting.

"I bet you travel first class all the way," she said, biting her lip.

He grinned. "Forget first class. We fly private."

***

There were no check-in queues or crowded gates. They drove through a security checkpoint right onto the runway, pulling up beside a small plane that stood ready and waiting. A customs officer greeted Rik and checked their passports, while the uniformed chauffeur dealt with their luggage.

"Enjoy your flight, sir," the customs officer said. Rik nodded and, with his hand in the small of her back, propelled her on board.

Kenzie had never been on a private plane before. It wasn't as big as she'd imagined, just one cabin with extra-large leather seats, an oversized entertainment system and a bathroom in the rear, but this under-stated elegance certainly beat flying cattle class any day.

"The trip's too short to require a hostess," Rik said once they were airborne, "but I can offer you champagne."

"Water will be fine, thanks."

She took the bottled water he offered and disappeared into the bathroom to get dressed. And to think she'd been worried about the acrobatics required to get into her cocktail dress inside an on-board loo. This bathroom was nearly as big as the one she shared with Lee.

An old fear had taken up residence in her stomach, squeezing like a tight fist, and she felt the urge to throw up again. She should have said no to Rik. Right now she should be tucked into bed with a bowl of chicken soup and Lauren Weisberger's new novel.

Why had she agreed to come? Because she was a sucker for a man in need. And because the chance to present the director with the palace in Neustadt as a film location was too good to refuse.

She splashed cold water on her face and examined her reflection in the mirror.

Because she'd wanted, desperately, madly, to see Rik again. Even though she knew it was the wrong thing to do, barely forty eight hours after she'd said goodbye, she wanted to take it all back. She'd done the one thing she'd vowed never to do again and fallen for the bad boy with the brooding eyes.

All he had to do was click his fingers and she came running. Just the way she'd done for her previous three boyfriends.

Her fringe fell across her face, and her bruised eyes and freckles stood out against her abnormally pale skin. What the hell had she been thinking?

This might be a party for friends and family, but she was never going to fit in. She remembered all too well the kind of people who socialised with royalty. Once upon a time they'd been her friends, until she'd really needed them and they'd abandoned her.

She swallowed hard. She also remembered the terror of walking into a party alone, while everyone whispered behind their hands. The last time she'd faced that ordeal, she'd had to do it alone. She would do anything in her power to make that moment easier for Rik.

Even if it meant sucking it up and facing the gauntlet of her worst fears.

With shaking hands, she applied her make-up. Though it had been years since she'd dolled herself up for this kind of party, she still remembered how to make the best of her features. At least she looked less freaky.

There was nothing she could do with her hair, though. Not without five hours, hot curlers and a stylist. So she brushed it smooth and left it hanging loose.

She looked nothing like that stylish blonde he'd been photographed with back in the days before his dethronement, but at least she shouldn't disappoint.

With her earrings in and her chin up she almost felt ready. She stepped out of the bathroom.

Her mouth turned dry.

"Wow," was all she managed to say.

Rik had changed too, into an elegant evening suit complete with black tie. With his new haircut and clean-shaven face he looked like a stranger. Or like James Bond.

"We'll have missed dinner by the time we get there. Do you want something to eat before we land?"

She shook her head. She couldn't face food right now.

"Then I suggest you buckle up. We'll be landing soon."

She crossed to her seat, and buckled herself in. Rik sat in the seat beside her. He smelled good too, though for a moment she wished he still smelled of the ocean. At least then he'd seem more familiar.

He still hadn't touched her, aside from that hand on her back as they boarded the plane, and her body seemed to have gone into some kind of withdrawal, yearning for his touch with an almost physical pain.

The plane landed smoothly, taxiing for what felt like forever before it finally came to a stop. She didn't move, even after Rik had unclasped his seatbelt and risen. Even after the door opened. He waited for her, hand outstretched. "The luggage will follow," he said.

Her stomach was so tied in knots she could barely stand. Would there be press waiting on the tarmac? Would they be bombarded by camera flashes the moment they stepped out? It seemed remarkably quiet out there.

She rose on shaky legs and moved to the door. Rik dropped his hand and preceded her down the stairs. She stepped out, the relief overwhelming when she saw that the runway was empty except for another sedan with tinted windows.

"Welcome to Westerwald," Rik said, holding the car door open for her.

The airport looked like any other, and the highway that carried them into the city of Neustadt could have been any highway. Darkness concealed the landscape, and then they were in the outskirts of the city, surrounded by warehouses and factories and ghostly office blocks. It was only when they reached the city centre that the place took on that otherwordly feel of a foreign place.

The capital city of Neustadt, as its name suggested, was relatively new by European standards, only a few hundred years old. It had the feeling of Paris, with broad tree-lined avenues, grand houses, and elegant storefronts. Then right in the heart of the old town, set back behind imposing railings, lay the palace. She'd seen photographs, of course, but none could beat the sight of its facade illuminated by soft uplights, a big moon hanging clear and bright and full overhead.

And then her heart contracted. There, unmistakeably, was her greatest fear. A phalanx of reporters and photographers pressed around the gate to which they were headed.

Their car might have darkened windows, but at the sight of dozens of flashbulbs popping, Kenzie slunk back in her seat. Her heart was beating so quickly she was sure it was about to take off like a rocket. And she felt an urge to throw up. Again.

The only thing that stopped her from puking all over the back of the luxury sedan was the clear and certain knowledge that somehow that would be the picture that would make tomorrow's headlines.

"Are you okay?" Rik asked.

She gritted her teeth. "I'd kill for that concierge's magic potion about now."

"And here I thought I'd be the one having the panic attack." He grinned.

"I don't like the press." Which was the under-statement of the century.

"They can't get any further than the gate," he re-assured her as the driver pulled up at the gate's security checkpoint. "Security around the palace is tight."

That still didn't diminish her urge to throw up. Or the black dots flickering before her eyes. Though perhaps that was the result of the camera flashes exploding as they nudged through the crowd.

At the last minute the intimidating wrought iron gates, with the Westerwald coat of arms picked out in gold scrollwork, slid open. Military guards stepped forward to hold back the surging crowd as the car drove through and the gates closed behind them.

Kenzie sighed out the breath she'd been holding.

There was still another set of gates, and another security checkpoint, before they rounded the palace building, passing out of sight of the press and into a gravel courtyard. The car pulled up beside a very ordinary looking side door that would have been unremarkable if it hadn't been flanked by two stocky men in black suits wearing those fancy earpieces that movie tough guys always wore.

How she wished Lee could see this.

One of the tough guys stepped forward and opened her car door.

This was it. Last chance to cower under the seat like a lunatic and ask the chauffeur to get her out of here at the speed of light.

Then Rik squeezed her hand and she remembered to breathe again. The dizziness passed. The nausea ebbed.

"You sure you're okay?" he asked again. "We don't have to go in if you don't want to."

What were her options? Going back to the flat in Shoreditch, to a cold, empty bed and the constant nausea she'd felt since she left Los Pajaros? Or a cold, empty bed in a hotel room in Warsaw?

Either way, she hadn't felt happy since she'd parted from Rik. Even if it was only tonight, and even if it meant smiling when she felt like crying, she wanted to be with him. When this ordeal was over, she planned to cuddle up to him and make love to him and pretend they were back in the tropics.

"Okay, let's do this," she said.

Chapter Thirteen

The tough guys had the side door open before they'd even stepped out the car. Rik barely glanced at the men flanking the doors as he strode inside and Kenzie had to hurry to keep up, which wasn't easy in heels. Then they were inside a large antechamber, and someone awaited them.

"You're late, bro," the Archduke said, engulfing his big brother in a hug.

"It's good to see you too."

The brothers were nothing alike. Where Rik was tall, dark and brooding, Max was all sunshine, fair-haired and smiling. He even had dimples. If his hair had been a little longer and shaggier, he'd have fitted in with those dive instructors on Christianstad no problem.

Kenzie was still struggling to take in the sight of two such gorgeous men in one eyeful when the door at the far end of the room opened and a young woman entered. Max let go of his brother and turned to her, and the look in his eyes told Kenzie exactly who she was – the bride to be.

She walked boldly, sass in every step. Up close she was stunning, with laughing eyes and tousled blonde hair. "Claus told me you'd arrived. I'm Phoenix, and you must be Rik."

Rik bent to give her a formal, polite kiss on her cheeks.

"This is Kenzie," he said, stepping back to draw her in.

In the presence of such a beauty, Kenzie would normally have felt like something the cat had thrown up, but then Phoenix smiled and looped an arm through hers, and her discomfort fled. "The party's in the Orangery. I don't know about you, but I could do with a drink."

Hell, yes.

"Kenzie's an unusual name," Phoenix observed, leading her out the antechamber and into a long gallery lined with portraits.

"No more than Phoenix is," Kenzie said, laughing a little. There was something about Phoenix that she made her instantly likable, instantly approachable.

"That's just a nickname. I loathe my given name." Phoenix sighed. "But I'm slowly getting used to answering to Georgiana." She made a face.

"Kenzie's short for Mackenzie. My mother was born a Mackenzie and she's very proud of her Scottish roots. I sometimes wonder what my parents were smoking when they named me."

Phoenix rolled her eyes. "Oh, I *know* what my parents were smoking." Unlike Kenzie, she sounded deadly serious.

The Orangery was at the rear of the building, a long conservatory with glass skylights and French doors that opened onto a formal garden. Kenzie could appreciate how the room lived up to its name. It was lined with potted orange trees, and though it was completely the wrong season, every tree seemed to be in blossom. She breathed in the scent that hung heavy in the air.

Rik stood beside her and breathed it in too. "My favourite scent," he said, taking her hand.

She was grateful for the anchor of his touch, because at that moment it was as though every conversation in the room ceased and every head in the room, nearly two hundred people, turned to look at them. Max and Phoenix scarcely seemed to notice, but Kenzie felt Rik stiffen beside her. She cast him a glance. He was formidable, every bit the regal prince.

Then he squeezed her hand, and she knew this wasn't as easy for him as it looked. This was what she was here for. So he could walk through this crowd as the guy with the pretty girl on his arm, looking for all the world as if he'd just interrupted a holiday to be here, rather than like the man who'd lost everything.

She could do that for him.

The crowd parted before them as they followed Max and Phoenix down the long room to the bar at the far end. The bar seemed incongruous in the space, a modern construction of mirrored glass and steel, reflecting every light in the room.

"Red or white?" the bow-tied barman asked.

"White." Kenzie recognised the label and glanced at Rik, raising an eyebrow. His eyes glinted and he smiled, and suddenly he was her pirate again and not some distant, intimidating stranger.

***

"The wine is from our grandfather's vineyard in California," Rik said. "It was one of Max's own blends from before he had to give up wine farming."

He watched as Kenzie raised the glass to her lips and took a sip. Then she ran her tongue along her lips, licking every last drop. There was no way she wasn't remembering just how much they'd both enjoyed this wine before.

"I almost thought you weren't coming. I was so pleased to get the call saying you'd requested a palace car at the airport." Max slung an arm around Rik's shoulder. "So you flew in from London – is that where you've been hiding all this time?"

Rik shook his head and dragged his eyes away from Kenzie's mouth. "I've been staying at Adam's place in the islands."

"The bastard! I asked him if you were there and he lied to my face and told me he had no idea where you were. Still, I take it he got my letter through to you? I'll have to thank him. He's around here somewhere."

Phoenix laughed. "Don't expect to see him any time soon. I saw him heading out into the gardens with a rather buxom brunette."

Rik glanced around the packed conservatory. Everywhere he looked there were familiar faces. A couple of cousins, friends of his and Max's from their school days, local aristocrats, and Westerwald's young and fabulous. He smiled at a familiar face – Claus, one of Max's closest friends from their childhood days.

The prickle of eyes on his back made him turn. His mother.

He would have thought she'd skip the more public part of the evening.

He turned quickly away.

"What is it?" Kenzie mouthed at him, concern in her eyes.

He looped his arm around her and pulled her close. He'd only shared two nights with her, yet her body moulded to his, familiar and comforting.

She looked past his shoulder. "Isn't she the reason you're here tonight?" she asked softly.

He shook his head but said nothing. Kenzie could have no clue that he was only here tonight because of her. He'd needed an excuse to chase after her, to keep her at his side. Once he'd searched her Facebook profile and read every tweet she'd ever written – which was plenty – he'd had a far better idea of what she wanted. And how he could get what he wanted.

She was a sucker for a person in need. All he'd had to do was give her a reason to feel needed. And that was easy. He did need her.

"I'm here for my brother," he said. "I have nothing left to say to her."

Kenzie pulled a little away from him. "No one understands mummy issues like I do, but you have to talk to her some time. She's still your mother."

"You want me to forgive her so we can all play happy families again?"

She shrugged. "Hey, I'm Switzerland in this. I just don't want you to have any regrets. All you have to do is listen. If you still feel you can't forgive her, then that's your choice."

"I'll talk to her." He buried his face in her hair. "But not tonight."

The party swirled about them. People stood in little groups talking, others dancing. The bright overhead lights of the chandeliers dimmed, replaced by swirling coloured lights which reflected in the glass-fronted bar. The room looked less like a formal room in a palace and more like a nightclub. Phoenix sure knew how to throw a party. There was no way Max had thought beyond what alcohol to serve.

The live band moved into the slow, seductive rhythm of a rumba.

"Let's dance," Rik suggested, turning her into his arms.

"I can't." Kenzie blushed. "Lee tried to teach me, but he says I'm useless at being led."

"That depends on who's doing the leading." He spun her into a dance hold, and began to move.

***

Kenzie had watched enough episodes of *Strictly Come Dancing* to know the most romantic of all dances wasn't easy. Yet somehow with Rik it did feel easy. Or perhaps that was simply because in his arms she felt lighter than air.

She was vaguely aware of other people beyond her vision, but they were mere shadows. None of them mattered. The only thing that mattered was that she was with Rik, dancing with him, touching him, pressed against him.

The way she'd wanted to be last night when she'd cried herself to sleep.

Only when the dance ended, did the rest of the room come back into focus.

"Ooh, you're good," she breathed.

He laughed, a low, sultry sound. "Say that again, louder so everyone can hear."

"As if you need compliments. You're arrogant enough already

without them."

"Am not!" His fingers skated down her back, tracing the line of her zip. Even through the fabric of her dress, the touch of his fingers sent a shiver through her.

"I missed you," he whispered.

She swallowed the catch in her throat. "It's only been a couple of days."

She'd missed him too. So much she'd even had a mad thought that it wasn't a stomach bug she'd picked up in the tropics, but that she'd felt sick because she wanted him so badly. Now that he was here, the nausea was history.

He took her hand in his and headed back towards the bar. "I need a refill. I'm thinking something with more of a kick in it than wine."

"A mojito?" she suggested, twinkling up at him.

They only made it halfway down the room before his attention was claimed by someone else. She ducked away and headed to the bar on her own.

"Two mojitos," she ordered, leaning against the bar. When the drinks were ready, she reached across the bar for them, then stepped back, onto someone's toes. "Oh I'm so sorry," she apologised, turning to her unintended victim.

"No harm, no foul," said the young woman beside her, with a smile that didn't quite reach her eyes.

Kenzie nearly dropped the glasses. The icy blonde was unmistakeable. She was even more beautiful in person than in the magazine photographs. Tall and willowy, with white blonde hair, peaches and cream skin, and eyes the colour of the Caribbean sky on a good day. She could have been a Scandinavian supermodel.

Rik's one and only girlfriend. The woman he'd planned to marry.

"You're Kenzie," the woman said.

Kenzie nodded. How on earth did she know?

The woman laughed, a tinkly, musical sound. "Everyone's been talking about you from the moment you walked in with Fredrik."

Of course. Kenzie felt the heat of a flush start to work its way up her neck. She really hadn't thought this whole date thing through properly. She'd assumed everyone would be talking about Rik, the prodigal son returned, and that she would be nothing more than an accessory. It hadn't occurred to her she might also be an object of interest.

She suddenly felt very exposed. And very scared.

"I'm Teresa Adler." The blonde held out a hand, and Kenzie fumbled to put the glasses down so she could shake it.

Teresa looked over Kenzie's shoulder to where Rik remained in conversation. "Fredrik looks more relaxed than I've ever seen him. He looks good."

She didn't sound possessive, or even particularly interested, but Kenzie's hackles still rose. *He's mine.*

But he wasn't.

It was only when Teresa moved to smooth back her already impeccably styled hair that Kenzie caught the glint on her finger. "You're engaged!"

Teresa smiled. "Yes, I am."

Well that was fast work. Kenzie didn't know whether to be pleased or offended on Rik's behalf.

Teresa stretched past Kenzie to take two flutes of champagne from the barman. "It was a pleasure meeting you, Kenzie." With another smile she glided off, an image of shimmering perfection.

Kenzie swallowed a large mouthful of mojito just as Rik disengaged himself from his conversation and came to her side.

"You met Teresa?" he asked.

She nodded. It was better he heard this from her now, than from someone else. "She's engaged."

"Good for her." Rik removed his glass from her fingers and took a sip.

"You're not upset?"

He frowned. "Should I be?"

She should have remembered he'd said he'd never been in love.

What hope in hell did she have of capturing Rik's heart when it hadn't been moved by that vision of perfection?

"I'm pleased for her," Rik said. "Teresa deserves to be happy."

Kenzie looked after Teresa's departing back. The one word she wouldn't have used to describe Teresa Adler was 'happy'. She didn't have the same glow that Phoenix had: the glow of a woman in love.

"We've shown our faces long enough," he said, his voice brushing her ear. "How about we take these drinks somewhere more private?"

She followed where he led, back along the gallery, then down a wide corridor with a high, vaulted ceiling. He pushed open a door, and she followed him in.

The room was dark. Rik moved away from her to flick on a switch and the warm yellow light of a standing lamp bathed the room in light. They stood in an office, dark wood-panelled walls, leather armchairs, and a massive mahogany desk bearing a state of the art desktop computer that looked dusty from lack of use. She'd never seen a desk look so neat, with the papers and books perfectly organised and even the pens lined up at right angles.

"It's untouched," Rik said, glancing around. "Max must be using our father's office then."

So this had been his space. His sanctum.

"Come here." Rik held out his hand, and when she took it he pulled her roughly against him. "I've wanted to do this all evening."

His hand found the zip at her back and eased it down.

"I thought you liked this dress?" she breathed.

"I do. But I like you out of it even better." He slid the sleeves down over her arms, and the dress fell in a puddle at her feet. His breath hitched.

He traced a hand over the sheer black lace covering her breasts. "You shouldn't have run from me in Los Pajaros."

No, she shouldn't have said 'yes' to him in London. But she wasn't about to dispute semantics right now, with his hands on her skin. The oh-so-sensible part of her brain had fled the moment

158

he kissed her beside the waterfall, and she was beginning to think it was gone for good.

She tilted her head back, exposing her neck to his kisses. When he drew back she opened half-lidded eyes.

With a wicked grin, Rik swept the books and papers aside. They tumbled onto the floor. Then he lifted her off her feet and onto her back on the desk.

Oh yes.

It might not be love. It might not be what she wanted or needed. But she would take any crumb Rik was willing to give her. And the sex was guaranteed to be so good she wouldn't care until it was too late.

***

A timid knock at the door brought Rik up through layers of sleep. Kenzie lay beside him, her top half bare, her long slim legs twisted in the duvet, her hair fanned out across the pillows. He smiled and pushed it back from her face. She didn't stir.

The knock came again. He pulled on his jogging bottoms and a long sleeved shirt and crossed to the door.

"Good morning, sir," Robert said as he opened the door. "I took the liberty of putting your coffee and papers in the morning room."

"Thank you, Robert." This was surreal. It was as if he'd never been away, as if the last four months had just been a bad dream. Except for the woman in his bed.

"I...um...thought you'd rather I didn't serve it in your room this morning."

"Good call." Rik shut the door softly behind him.

"There are some outstanding papers for you to sign, and a few other issues that need to be attended to. Phoenix has offered to give Ms Cole the grand tour of the state apartments for her photographs while you're busy with the Private Secretary."

"Thank you. Where are my brother and his lovely bride-to-be

this morning?"

"They went out for a bike ride but should be back soon. Is there anything else you require, Your Highness?"

Rik shook his head. "I have no claim to that title anymore."

Robert lifted his chin. "Within these grounds you will always remain Your Highness. Besides, I've called you that since you were in your teens. How else should I address you?"

"You could call me Rik". He laughed at the affronted look on his valet's face. "Thank you, Robert. You can tell the Secretary I'll be with him in an hour."

He returned to the bedroom to wake Kenzie. He didn't want to waste even another ten minutes without her.

He'd realised something incredible during the party last night and he wanted to share it with her. Perhaps not now, with matters of state to be dealt with and her location pictures to be taken, but later, when they had all the time in the world.

He stroked a hand down her back and watched goose bumps rise beneath his fingers. Then she murmured, opened her eyes, and smiled at him. And the rest of the world just had to wait.

***

What did one wear to breakfast with royalty? Kenzie hadn't exactly packed for a palace stay, so jeans and her favourite green cashmere sweater would just have to do. The sweater was a Christmas gift from Lee who had a more than passing interest in fashion, so it fitted way better than her usual clothes. She brushed her hair back into a ponytail and joined Rik in the morning room for coffee.

He was already dressed, in grey trousers, with a buttoned-up shirt and charcoal sweater. He couldn't have looked more preppy if he tried. "I would do anything to see you out in public in short sleeves," she said, pouring coffee from the antique-looking silver coffee pot into a dainty porcelain cup. "Or better yet, shirtless."

She glanced around the sitting room which resembled a spread from a Condé Nast magazine. "Do you have an afternoon room too?"

Rik grinned and patted his knee, inviting her over. "It's called the morning room because it faces east and gets the morning light. Normally I'd have my breakfast alone in here, but with a house full of guests, breakfast will be served in the dining room."

She sat on his lap and brushed back a lock of hair from his eyes. He'd found time to shave this morning. She missed the roughened stubble and too long hair, but it certainly made kissing him far more pleasurable. At least she wouldn't have to face all the other house guests sporting stubble burn.

"I have some work to do, but after breakfast Phoenix will take you around the palace so you can get your photographs. Then you can use my office computer to upload the pictures."

She looked down at the cup in her hands. "Rik...we need to talk."

He laid a finger over her lips. "Not now. We can talk later."

***

Max and Phoenix were already at breakfast, alone in the massive dining room that looked more like a film set than a real life room. Kenzie breathed a sigh of relief to see that none of the other house guests had yet emerged. She was equally relieved to see that both the Archduke and his fiancée wore jeans.

"You don't look as if you partied all night," Kenzie commented, helping herself to breakfast from the buffet.

Phoenix grinned. "As long as I stay away from champagne, I never get drunk."

While they ate, Rik plied his brother with questions about new policies that were under debate, and how Max was getting on with the prime minister, until Phoenix threw her hands in the air. "You're giving me indigestion. If you want to work, take it to the office and leave us in peace."

They did as they were told, and as soon as they were alone,

Phoenix turned to Kenzie with a smile. "So tell me – how did you and Rik meet?"

"*He picked me up in a bar,*" didn't sound quite right. Nor did "*He was drunk and I let him sleep in my bed rather than being arrested.*" So she went with door number three, the sanitised version: "He helped me scout for locations for a film shoot."

"Was it love at first sight?"

Kenzie choked on her toast. "Lust at first sight, maybe. Rik and I...love doesn't come into it."

Kenzie squirmed beneath Phoenix's sceptical gaze. She was grateful when the door opened to reveal a bleary-eyed house guest. For about half a second.

"Adam Hatton?"

Of all the baroque palaces in all the world, he had to walk into this one.

Charlie's best friend.

He looked up, rubbing the back of his neck, and it was a moment before recognition dawned in his eyes. Followed immediately by something that looked a lot like loathing.

If she could have crawled under the table and hidden from sight, she would have. But with Phoenix's curious gaze flitting between them, she straightened her shoulders and forced a smile. Then with limbs so stiff she could hardly walk, she rose from her chair. "If you'll excuse me, I need to fetch my camera." The nausea was back, stronger than before.

Phoenix nodded. "I'll meet you at the main staircase in ten."

Kenzie fled.

Chapter Fourteen

Kenzie folded the gift wrap and stuck it down with trembling fingers. She'd managed to keep a smile on her face and to chat with Phoenix as they'd gone from one state room to another, but her feet had felt like lead and her mouth had been too dry, and she was sure Phoenix knew something was wrong.

The clues had all been there. How had she not put them together?

Adam lived in Hertfordshire. His family's pile wasn't that many miles from her own childhood home. Rik had been to The Waffle House.

Adam's family owned a holiday home in the Caribbean. She'd never known exactly where, but he'd kept a yacht there.

They both played polo.

She should have made the connection.

And she really should have Googled Rik rather than trying to pretend he wasn't who he was. That was the least she would do for a job, yet somehow the thought never even occurred to her when it came to her love life. A therapist would have a field day with that.

And even without Google, she should have known that everyone in that circle, the wealthy, the titled, they all knew each other. And they stuck together, while she was just an outsider.

Now it was merely a matter of time before they talked and

that past she'd tried so hard to outrun caught up with her again.

With extra care she twined ribbon around the package and tied a bow. She'd bought this gift for him on her walk home from the tube station after the long flight. At first she'd thought she'd been jet-lagged and hadn't believed her eyes as she'd looked in the window of the hospice shop. She'd planned to mail it to Rik, but since he'd shown up at her door she'd decided to give it to him in person. Phoenix had supplied the paper and tape, and Kenzie prayed it would help ease the inevitable conversation.

The door opened and her heart contracted, but it wasn't Rik. Not yet.

"I'm sorry," his mother said. "I was hoping to find Rik here."

"He's downstairs with Max."

It was obvious that Archduchess Anna had been a beauty in her youth. She still had the bone structure and the figure. But aside from the eyes, that same midnight blue shade as Rik's, there was very little resemblance between them. However, Max was definitely his mother's child.

Anna closed the door and crossed the room to her side. "Are you okay?"

Everyone kept asking her that. Couldn't they see she wasn't okay? Kenzie swallowed and nodded. "I'm fine. I've just got a bit of a tummy bug. I think I picked it up in Los Pajaros."

Anna perched on the edge of the sofa beside her, her hands folded demurely in her lap. But the way her knuckles turned white gave away her tension. "Has Rik forgiven me?"

How the hell should I know? But Kenzie bit her tongue. "I don't know."

"Will he speak to me?"

This was what happened when you let someone in. You landed up *involved*, slap bang in the middle of someone else's issues. Kenzie squirmed. "I'm sure he will." She hoped.

"He hates me."

"He doesn't hate you."

Anna looked down at her hands. "The last time I saw him, he said 'I hate you'."

"People say things they don't mean when they're angry." Adam had said a lot of things when he was angry too. She hoped he'd calmed down since then.

"He hasn't returned my calls for nearly four months."

"He needed time. I gather he hasn't done much of anything these last few months, but he's here now and that must mean something."

Anna's head came up, the look in her eyes sharp. "What do you mean you 'gather?' How long have you known Rik?"

"About a week."

The older woman's eyes opened wide. Which at least proved that her lack of wrinkles was completely natural. She'd never have managed such a stunned expression with Botox. "You've known Rik a week and he brought you home to meet the family? And you're staying here in his rooms. I assumed he'd known you for months. He's usually very careful that way."

Oh great. So she was just the mistake he'd made when he stopped being careful? She could only pray Rik didn't agree. Especially after he heard whatever Adam had to say.

She needed to get to him first. She needed to be the one to tell him what happened with Charlie all those years ago.

But she wasn't the only one who needed to talk to Rik. Watching this composed woman, as dignified as a queen, twisting her hands in her lap, Kenzie's heart went out to her. His mother had a much bigger claim. "You might find him in his office," she said.

Anna smiled. "Thank you." She rose, with a grace Kenzie couldn't hope to emulate, and walked to the door. "I hope we have a chance to get to know each other better."

You and me both. Because if she was still around to get to know his family better, then it meant he hadn't given her the boot. Strange that three days ago she'd been ready to walk away from Rik, sure it was the best thing to do.

Now, the thought of never seeing him again was like a physical blow to her chest. Absence really did make the heart grow fonder, even if it was only a matter of hours.

She would make this right between them. She'd go to Rik's office and she'd tell him everything. The whole sordid story, even the things she'd never told another living soul.

Everything always worked out in the end. She had to believe that.

But first she'd give his mother half an hour with him. And pray that by the time they were done his mood wasn't wrecked.

***

Rik returned to his own office, relieved to leave Max to his job. Considering he'd had no hand-over whatsoever, Max had done a remarkable job picking up the pieces. Almost as though he'd been born to it. Who'd have thought his easygoing little brother would have had an aptitude for running the country?

He grinned. And for keeping the prime minister in check.

He surveyed the wreckage of his desk and began to right the mess he and Kenzie had made last night. Most of this stuff could be binned, anyway. It wasn't like he'd need any of it where he was going. Surprisingly, he didn't feel even the least regret.

He'd spent so many hours within this room, closed in, out of the sun, often late at night when the day's meetings and parliamentary sessions were done. The room smelled musty now. He longed for the fresh, clean air of Los Pajaros. And the freedom to bare his skin to the sun.

Time and distance really could work miracles. Or maybe it was Kenzie who'd wrought the miracle.

He started to sort through the papers as a knock sounded on the door. Kenzie. He smiled in welcome, his entire body electrified at the mere thought of seeing her again.

"Come in," he called, and the door swung open. Instant buzz kill. "Hello, Mother."

"Do you have a moment for me?"

He'd promised Kenzie he'd listen. So he sat on the edge of the desk, arms crossed over his chest, and nodded.

His mother stepped into the room and closed the door behind her. She didn't take a seat, but hovered, uncertain of her welcome. He'd never seen her at such a loss, even on that night he'd confronted her in her rooms in Waldburg with the results of his DNA test.

"I'm listening," he said.

"I hoped you'd forgive me by now."

"For what – for lying to me about who I am all my life? For lying to the man you claimed to love? Or for sleeping around before you married my... your husband?" He choked on that last word. It was still impossible to think of Christian von Waldburg as anything but his father.

"We all make mistakes, Rik. None of us are perfect." She drew in a deep breath. "Even your father. You idolised him, but he kept his own secrets too."

"Which father would that be – the drunken tryst in a nightclub, or the prince?"

She levelled her gaze on him. "You only ever had one father."

Rik cleared his throat and voiced the one thing that weighed most heavily on him. "I thought you loved him. How could you keep this secret from him?"

"I kept my secret *because* I loved him. He was so excited when he realised I was pregnant, and he wanted you so much. I didn't have the heart to take that from him." Her eyes glazed with unshed tears. "He would have loved you just the same, no matter whose son you were, and he would have treated you the same as he treated Max. But he was also an honourable man. He would not have raised you as his heir had he known the truth." She sighed. "The world was a very different place thirty-five years ago. Christian might have treated you as his son, but the rest of the world would have seen you as a bastard. I wanted to protect you from that. But you're a grown man now. You can handle the truth." A single tear slid down her cheek. "You'll perhaps never truly understand this, but a mother loves her child so much she'll do absolutely anything to protect it. Even lie to the man she loves."

Kenzie had understood.

He pushed away from the desk to pace the room.

"You had to know the truth would come out eventually. You knew the law required a DNA test before my accession could be ratified by the government."

She nodded. "And I knew the test would only be done after your father's death, when the truth could no longer hurt him."

"But it hurt me."

She straightened her shoulders and looked him in the eye. "It made you."

He stopped pacing to stare at her.

"You are a fine man, Rik, and I'm proud of you but you also have a tendency to think too much and to take life too seriously. As Archduke you would have done your duty but you would have died inside. You were fast on your way to becoming a real bore."

She stepped closer, laying a hand on his arm. He didn't shrug it off. "I've never seen you more relaxed than you were last night, in spite of everything. For the first time, you didn't care what anyone else thought, you simply let yourself go."

He remembered that devastating dance with Kenzie, the way she'd felt in his arms. The way he'd taken her away from the party without a care as to who saw them leave. The way he'd taken her right here on this desk. He had let go with her, over and over again.

As if sensing where his thoughts strayed, his mother smiled. "You never once looked at Teresa the way you look at Kenzie."

Probably because he'd never once felt the urge to lay Teresa across his desk, unable to endure another moment without being inside her.

"I like her. She brings out your impulsive side." This time his mother's smile lit her eyes. She looked lighter.

"I plan to tell her today that I love her."

Perhaps only his mother would understand what a big deal this was. Or Kenzie.

He grinned. He was done with putting this off. He needed to talk to her *now*.

His mother looked up at him, with those eyes that mirrored his own. "Are we ok?"

He nodded. "We're ok."

With a bounce in her step, she headed toward the door, blowing him a kiss as she left the room. He smiled. When they were children, his mother had tucked him into bed every night, and every night she'd blown him a kiss from the door.

That single kiss wiped out every doubt he'd struggled with these last few months. He'd been loved. His mother hadn't lied to save herself. She'd lied because she loved him. Perhaps sometimes the end did justify the means.

He felt lighter too. Kenzie was right, and he was glad he'd agreed to listen. She must surely have finished taking her photographs by now. She should be here at any moment to upload them. Then...

He heard voices outside in the corridor, his mother greeting someone as they passed. He hurried to the door and opened it wide. But it wasn't Kenzie.

Adam, his old uni friend and the owner of the guesthouse he'd been crashing in the last few months.

Sheesh. He'd hardly had this many visitors when he'd been Archduke in training.

He managed a grin, even as he glanced over Adam's shoulder to look for Kenzie. "Hey there, I missed you last night. I gather it had something to do with a brunette? Some things never change."

Adam thumped him on the shoulder in greeting. "And you left the party early. Some things do change."

He flopped into the leather armchair, and Rik followed to sit on the edge of the desk again. He left the door ajar so he could listen for Kenzie. "I really appreciate that you've let me stay in your villa so long. I'll clear out of there soon."

"No need. Stay as long as you like. The place is just standing empty anyhow." Adam lounged back in the chair. "And my offer stands if you're getting bored of the islands. You have that first in economics and you're welcome to a job with us any time you want."

Investment banking. It wouldn't be so bad if Adam's family didn't own the company. But to be the outsider in someone else's family business... the contrast with his own family business would be too stark.

Besides, the thought of swapping this office for another held little appeal. Kenzie was right. He had the chance to be anything, do anything...

He grinned. "Thanks, but I think I'm a little old to retrain. I plan to stay on in Los Pajaros."

"What — ferry tourists around the islands and get lucky with the pretty ones? I'm really pleased you're starting to live it up at last, but you'll be bored stiff."

The thought of getting lucky with anyone but Kenzie held zero appeal. And there was no chance he'd grow bored. Not as long as he had her at his side to challenge him.

But as much as Adam was one of his closest friends — as close as one could be when they'd lived in separate countries since their uni days — Rik wasn't ready to share his revelation. He wanted Kenzie to be the first to hear it.

Adam leaned forward in his seat, his face suddenly serious. "There's something you should know about your date."

"What is it?"

"She used to date Charlie."

It took Rik a moment to place the name. Charles St Aubyn had played polo with them in their Oxford days. He and Adam had been good friends. "Is there anyone in England Charlie didn't date?"

"Not like that. They were serious."

A knot formed in Rik's stomach. He didn't like the thought of Kenzie with anyone else, and as for Charlie — he'd been a thoughtless, selfish playboy with more money than brains. If she'd dated him, it was no wonder Kenzie had ended up hurt. And it would explain her issues with trust fund wastrels.

"She's the one who..." Adam's voice trailed off.

Rik frowned. "Who what?"

***

Outside in the corridor, Kenzie paused at the sound of voices coming from inside the office. Then she recognised Adam's voice. "Kenzie's the one who was with Charlie when he shot himself."

She couldn't feel anything from the neck down. She couldn't move, couldn't get away. It was happening again. No matter where she went, no matter what she did, the poison spread, and she was unable to escape it.

Inside the room, Rik said nothing.

Adam hadn't finished. "She destroyed the note he left. Or at least that's what she told the inquest. But she refused to say what was in the letter or why he did it." He dug the knife in deeper. "Rumour had it Charlie didn't commit suicide at all. Maybe she killed him and made it look like suicide."

Kenzie pressed her eyes closed. She didn't need Adam's voice to remind her what had happened. She relived the ordeal often enough as it was. Usually every time she sat down in a job interview with a prospective boss. *Oh, that's where I heard the name...I remember now, it was all over the press.*

And the press had been all over her.

It didn't matter that the police hadn't found anything suspicious. There'd been enough evidence to support the suicide theory and they'd closed the files. But Charlie's family had wealth and influence. They'd tried to bribe her into revealing the contents of that suicide note, and when she refused they dragged her into court and fed rumour and innuendo to the tabloids who'd lapped up every whiff of scandal.

171

The story still surfaced every now and then, thankfully only on the back pages these days, and only on slow news days, but that was enough to keep the memory alive.

Rik still hadn't said anything. Her chest pulled so tight it ached. Why wasn't he saying anything? It was like that moment back on Isla Corona, when she'd admitted to knowing who he was, only a hundred times worse.

"I know how you feel about scandal," Adam said. "I thought you should know. Especially now with all the secrets coming out in your family."

And there it was. The reason she'd rather pretend he was a pirate than a prince. The reason she'd walked away from Rik on that pier in Los Pajaros. The reason she should have said 'no' to temptation in London.

There was no way this could ever end well.

The hot burn of tears brought her limbs to life. She turned and walked away the way she'd come.

Sod 'everything always working out in the end.' How many times did she have to bang her head against a brick wall before she realised that maybe things didn't work out, no matter how many back up plans you made? No matter if you thought this time would be different, or you'd finally left the past behind, or that this time your heart wouldn't be trampled.

She climbed the grand stairs to the private apartments, barely able to see through the sheen of tears.

Rik had made it clear he wanted to indulge himself for as long as this chemistry lasted. He'd offered her an extra week on Los Pajaros. What were the chances he'd want her now that he knew? What were the chances he'd stand by her when her mere presence in the palace could bring more scandal?

He hadn't said a word.

The least she could do was leave. Now. While she could still walk out the door with a modicum of dignity. While she could still hold her head high.

Chapter Fifteen

Rik levelled his gaze on Adam. "Rumour says a lot of things. Did you ask Kenzie for her side of the story?"

Adam shrugged. "She refused to talk at the inquest and she refused to talk to Charlie's parents."

Refusing to talk was a lot different from being culpable.

Rik remembered the story. Having known Charlie, of course he'd followed the press coverage until it got repetitive. He'd been surprised it was a suicide. With Charlie's reputation with women he'd been sure it would be a jealous husband who'd get him in the end.

"Thank you for telling me." Rik rose, desperate now to get away, to find Kenzie.

This certainly made sense of her anxiety as they'd passed through the media frenzy at the palace gates the night before. He'd lived in the spotlight his whole life and he still found it invasive. How much more so would it have been for Kenzie?

He came close to giving Adam a shove out the door in his eagerness to get moving.

"Good to see you again, mate," Adam said. "You're looking so much happier. Looks like your holiday in the islands has been good for you."

No, Kenzie had been good for him. Rik mounted the stairs of the grand staircase two at a time, almost crashing into a housemaid's trolley in the corridor outside his suite. He shoved open the door. Where the hell was she? Surely she couldn't still be photographing the state apartments?

He poked his head into the bedroom.

Her suitcase was gone.

He hurried through the apartment, reaching the morning room, where his anxious gaze found the gift-wrapped parcel on the coffee table. There was no note, but it could only be meant for him.

He ripped the ribbon off, and tore the paper. A large hardcover book of wildlife photographs. He frowned. It wasn't even a new book. It looked used, the cover a little torn, the pages yellowed at the edges.

He opened the cover and inside, in Kenzie's large, rounded hand was an inscription.

Only that which is the other gives us fully unto ourselves. – Sri Yogananda.

What the hell did that mean?

He turned the page to the cover plate, and his heart stopped. He couldn't breathe. His hand stroked down the page, over the bold lettering announcing the photographer's name: Robert Ellis.

It was the dedication that made everything clear and brought the air whooshing back into his lungs. *My passion. My labour of love. My reason for being.*

The fashion photographer might have been a womaniser in a vain and frivolous line of work, but he'd also had hidden depths. Rik flicked through the pages. Glossy close-up pictures of birds and lizards and animals. He paused at the double page spread of a sea turtle laying her eggs in the white sand of a pristine beach.

Tears welled in his eyes.

Perhaps there was more of his father in him than he'd realised. Of both fathers. And perhaps he could live the passion that his natural father never had.

He snapped the book shut and set it down on the table. *Make a difference in the world*, Kenzie had told him.

Where the hell was she?

***

@KenzieCole101: @ProducerNeil I have pictures. Not Warsaw but I think you'll be very happy.

@ProducerNeil: @KenzieCole101 When can we see them?

@KenzieCole101: @ProducerNeil If there's wireless on train to Brussels I'll send from there. If not I'll send from Eurostar. I'm booked on the last one out.

@LeeHill: @KenzieCole101 Why the hell you coming back so soon?

@KenzieCole101: @LeeHill Can't talk now. Have a train to catch.

With minutes to spare, Kenzie tossed her last Euros at the bemused taxi driver and dashed into the terminal. She'd bet anything he'd never collected a fare from the back gate of the palace before. She had a fleeting impression of a vast domed roof painted with a vivid mural, and gothic architecture, all columns and pointy windows. She had no more time than that to admire the scenery.

She found an automatic ticket machine, selected a one-way ticket home and swiped her credit card.

Platform five. Train departing in two minutes.

She set off at a run, her wheelie case skidding and sliding on the grey tiled floor.

She needn't have bothered.

As she passed platform four the announcement came over the tinny speakers, repeated in at least five different languages. It didn't matter which language she heard it in, the news was still crap: train delayed.

Just her damn luck.

She slowed her mad dash and swallowed a hiccup. Forget Warsaw. Forget her job. She wanted to go home and she wanted to go home *now*. If she didn't make that connection to the last Eurostar train from Brussels, she wouldn't get home until tomorrow.

Hot tears burned her eyes and she brushed them away. Not yet. She wouldn't let them fall until she reached home. Not until she was behind a locked door with furniture to kick and a pillow to weep into.

Every seat on the platform was already occupied, by passengers who looked either bored or annoyed. And one businessman, irritatedly fluffing up his broadsheet as the baby beside him squealed, looked both.

This was a far cry from the trip she'd made into Westerwald. No more private planes, just back to reality with a very hard bump for Mackenzie Cole.

Same old, same old.

She plopped her case down on the platform, sank onto it and buried her face in her hands. She needed a good cry. Crying on a suitcase. She belonged in a sad country song.

Nope. She had to hold back the tears. Hers wasn't a face that could cry prettily. Tears turned her pale skin splotchy.

If this were a film, right now the violins would be playing, and the hero would be running in slow motion across the airport – or train station – to stop the woman of his dreams from leaving. But life wasn't like the movies. It was about time she accepted that. Life didn't have soaring violins and happy ever afters.

Life was messy and complicated, and relationships meant nothing but heartbreak. Roll on the thirty cats, because she was never, ever going to let another man into her heart again.

She only looked up when an ear-piercing squeal announced

the train's arrival. It slid in beside the platform and threw open its doors, as if it couldn't wait to disgorge its current passengers and get going again.

Which exactly mirrored her feeling.

In no mood to fight the crowds, she stayed on her suitcase until the waiting passengers had pushed and shoved their way on board. Then she made her way towards the emptiest compartment she could find and manhandled her case across the gap and up the giant step onto the train. She paused, casting a look back over her shoulder at the rapidly emptying platform.

If this were a film, then any moment now the doors at the far end of the platform – not that there were any, just a steel turn-stile – would burst open and Rik would appear. They would run towards each other in slow motion and there would be tears and declarations of true love.

The conductor's shrill whistle split the air, the doors began to beep, and Kenzie leapt up behind her case just as the doors swished closed. She leaned back against them and heaved out a sigh. The last bit of hope she'd obstinately clung to fled with her breath and the tears refused to stay back.

By now Rik must have found her gift. And still he hadn't come after her.

It was well and truly over.

Meanwhile, Rik elbowed his way through the crowd in the terminal. After the peace and quiet and sedentary ways of Los Pajaros, this shoving crowd of passengers, too wrapped up in their own thoughts to even notice him, was an extraordinary culture shock. Not that he'd ever had to fight his way through a crowd before. In the past, people had tended to make way for him. Though perhaps the intimidating bodyguards had something to do with that. How he wished for a man in black with dark glasses and an earpiece right now.

Then he was through the crowd and the sign for platform

five, *Departures to Brussels*, was in sight. He barrelled through the turnstile just as the train doors closed. Not caring how much of a fool he looked, he ran down the platform as the train began to hiss and move. He waved his arms. "Arrete! Halt! Stop!"

People peered out the windows at him as if he were some lunatic. But none of the faces turning to look were the one he wanted to see.

The train picked up speed, hissing ominously, and he chased it until he ran out of platform and the last carriage rolled past him.

For the first time in his life he felt the urge to use the F word.

Rik stood at the very edge of the platform, chest heaving, and watched the train's red taillights disappear from sight. His chest burned as the adrenalin rush waned.

Think.

Even though the train would take three hours to reach Brussels, in rush hour traffic he'd never make it there before her.

If he had a plane ready fuelled and waiting, he might just be able to make it to London ahead of her. But he'd released the charter plane, and in a move to improve the palace's carbon footprint, Max had done away with the royal plane.

As his breathing returned to normal, Rik's brain finally caught up. The airforce.

He fetched his mobile from his pocket and pressed speed dial. He was still breathless when the call was answered. "Hi little brother. Remember that favour you said you owed me? I'd like to call it in."

***

@ProducerNeil: @KenzieCole101 Got the pics. Incredible. If you want a job on JJ's film, you got it!

@KenzieCole101: @ProducerNeil I'll think about it.

The train slowing brought Kenzie out of her doze. She rubbed her eyes and stretched, her limbs cramped from sitting in one place too long. Through the windows, London's gritty landscape shifted into focus. Grey sky, grey buildings.

Around her the other passengers hurried to gather their baggage, eager to reach their destinations.

Eager definitely wasn't how she felt. Hollow. Numb. Dead. Those were better words.

What did she have to go home to anyway?

She'd achieved everything she set out to achieve. She'd secured locations for this film that the director had only dreamed of. She'd earned the respect of the film's production team. She already had the next job lined up.

She wasn't a screw up any more. And even if no-one else recognised that, she knew it now.

But it all felt like nothing beside the hole in her heart.

She'd left the most incredible man she'd ever met behind. Rik wasn't broken. He didn't need fixing. And she was sure, with every fibre of her being, that he was the man she'd been looking for. But she couldn't be selfish. It would be better for him and for his family if she stayed far away.

She'd made tough decisions before. She'd faced worse than a broken heart, and she'd survived that. She could survive this decision too.

The train rolled into St Pancras International and the other passengers began to push and shove to reach the doors. The voices around her increased in volume. And there was music playing in the station. Violins.

The train jerked to a stop. Kenzie stood and reached for her case and heaved it from the rack. On the other side of the carriage everyone suddenly seemed to be pressing their noses up against the windows.

"Look at that!"

"I wonder what they're advertising?"

The voices filtered through the fug in her brain and she twisted around to see what the commotion was about. But all she could see was the backs of heads.

The carriage doors swooshed open, and the sound of the violins grew louder. She bit her lip. It was the same song she and Rik had danced the rumba to last night. It was surreal. Like she'd stepped into a film and could hear the soundtrack playing.

Long moments passed before the queue of eager beavers had thinned enough for her to see through the windows to the platform.

Her heart did a little jump. Frangipanis in London in October? Short-lived as those flowers were, these had to be plastic. They were mounted on a trellis, forming letters at least four feet high. From where she stood she could make out the word 'LOVE'.

Wasn't this just great? As if her life wasn't already sucky enough, the universe had decided to mock her too. She averted her eyes and headed for the carriage doors.

She bumped her suitcase down to the platform, and turned to join the bottleneck to leave the platform. The sweet frangipani scent was real. Someone had spent a lot of money on this promotion. She breathed it in and tears pricked her eyes as memories flooded her.

Now the full wording of the floral letters was visible: *I love you.*

Three words she never expected to hear from the person she loved more than any other. The man who made every other man who'd passed through her life nothing more than a shadow.

The reason for the bottleneck became clear as she reached the escalators heading down to the arcade. Her fellow passengers trickled past a band at the bottom of the escalator. No, not a band. A small orchestra.

It was past nine o'clock. Surely the station wasn't busy enough to warrant such a big advertising promotion this late on a weeknight?

She stepped onto the escalator. She didn't feel up to fighting the tube system with a big suitcase in tow. What were the chances the production office would allow her to claim the cost of a taxi on her expenses?

As the escalator descended, her eyes widened. Between the obligatory station patisserie and the exit to the taxi rank a dance had broken out. There had to be at least a dozen couples dancing the rumba.

"It's a flash mob," the woman in front of her said.

A super organised flash mob to provide its own orchestra, Kenzie thought. Or perhaps she was still asleep on the train and dreaming. She squeezed her eyes shut. But when she opened her eyes, the dream hadn't changed.

And that was when she noticed the man standing at the bottom of the escalator.

Rik.

He hadn't even taken time to change. He still wore that preppy sweater over the high-collared shirt. He grinned as he spotted her. And he pulled the sweater off over his head.

She'd reached the bottom of the escalator and stepped off. And there she stayed, her heart in her throat, torn between laughing and crying.

Rik began to undo the buttons of his shirt. Kenzie couldn't move a muscle. "What on earth are you doing?"

"This morning you said you'd do anything to see me shirtless in public. Your wish is granted."

He'd reached the last button.

People stopped trying to push past her. She couldn't blame them for stopping to gawk, but it was enough to galvanise her. Before he could go any further, she pulled him away from the grinning spectators.

"What are you doing here?" she managed.

"You said we needed to talk this morning and I agreed. Since you decided to leave before we could, I thought I'd catch you here."

"You arranged all of this?" She blinked. *For me? Why?* Then she remembered the flowers. *I love you.*

Oh my God.

"Where did you find the flowers?"

"I didn't. Your friend Lee recommended a props buyer who had a contact who... I've just chased you halfway across Europe and you want to talk about flowers?"

He stooped to pick up his discarded sweater. "We can't talk here." Handing her suitcase to a uniformed man who looked remarkably like the chauffeur who'd driven them to the airport yesterday, he led her away from the band and the dancers.

She followed, too dumbstruck to resist. He shouldn't be here. This was a public place – what if anyone saw them together? What if he was photographed with her?

She would never forgive herself if she tainted his reputation.

"You shouldn't be doing this," she said, struggling to keep up with him.

"Why – is it too much?"

He knew that wasn't what she meant.

He led her back upstairs to the champagne bar. Not to the public bar, the world's longest champagne bar, but to a private lounge, she noted with relief. A private lounge that smelled of frangipani. Two glasses of champagne sat ready and waiting for them. Kenzie resisted the urge to grab a glass and gulp it down.

"Are you mad?" she asked, turning to him. "You shouldn't even be here."

He took her face in his hands. "There is no place else in the world I want to be except where you are. Come back to Los Pajaros with me.

She couldn't look away.

"I love you, Kenzie."

She shook her head. "But Adam told you..."

His eyes narrowed. "So that's why you ran?" he released her face and pushed his hands through his hair. "We all have a past. And you know what I've learned? We can't go back there. We have to move forward."

"But you have to know..."

He laid a finger across his lips. "I don't have to know anything. You can keep your secrets and we can still be happy together. My parents managed as much. I'll still love you, no matter what happened in the past."

Tears blinded her. "But I want to tell you. I don't want to keep any secrets from you."

He sat on a plush suede sofa and pulled her down into his lap.

She blinked away the tears. She'd never felt as safe as she did now, in his arms. And she was tired of keeping this to herself, tired of running, tired of carrying this alone. His shoulders had been big enough to carry the weight of a nation. He was strong enough to share just a little of her burden. "Charlie was the most fun person I ever met, so adventurous and full of life, but I always knew he was broken inside. I was still naïve enough then to think I could fix him. I thought giving him the love and the family he'd never known would make everything okay. But I couldn't fix him, and it's my fault he's dead. The day I told him I was pregnant with his child, he snapped. He killed himself. Do you know why he did it?"

Rik said nothing.

Her throat was so choked she could barely speak. "He said he wanted a better life for his child. He didn't want his child growing up with a father like him." She brushed her sleeves across her eyes. "I destroyed his note. I didn't want anyone else to know."

At least Rik hadn't let her go. She looked up into his eyes. He was doing his mask thing again.

"You had his child?"

She shook her head. "With all the stress of the inquest and the civil trial and the press... I lost the baby at just over four months. It was a girl."

He continued to hold her, his hand stroking down her back. "You wanted that baby?"

"So much it hurt." She looked away.

"You have a kind heart, Kenzie, and you didn't deserve the pain

183

Charlie caused you. But if it's any consolation, the Charlie I knew didn't think of anyone but himself. Troubled as he was, he must have really loved you to feel so deeply."

He wiped a tear away from her cheek. "You have that effect on me too. I'm starting to understand how it feels to want something so badly it hurts. Because there's something I want desperately. Passionately."

She looked up at him. His fingers traced down her cheek and brushed her lips.

"I love you more than I have ever loved anything in my life. I love you more than I love my country. I can breathe without my country, but I can't breathe without you. You've been in love before, so you know how this feels, but for me this is a big deal."

If anyone had ever told her a broken heart could be made whole with just a few sentences, she'd never have believed it. She did now.

"You're wrong," she said.

He stiffened. His brow furrowed and the mask slipped. Incredulity. Fear. He was afraid she was going to tell him she didn't love him back. As if. "You're wrong to think that I've been in love before. Because all those times I thought I loved someone, was nothing to what I feel right now. Nothing."

"So you'll come back to Los Pajaros with me?"

In a heartbeat. Even if it was only one week. But her instincts didn't think a week would be enough, or a year...

"As long as I'm not just your back up plan."

He grinned. "No, you're part of the new, improved, much-better-than-the-original plan."

She slid off his lap and held out her hands to him. "Okay, I'm sold. Let's go home."

"And where is that?"

Her eyes misted over again, but this time they were tears of joy. "Where the sun always shines, and the sea is warm, and where bright tropical birds flit through the trees."

"What about your career?"

"I've been thinking about that five year plan thing of yours. I think I have one."

"Yes?"

"In five years' time I'd like to be running a film commission in Los Pajaros. There are so many beautiful, unspoilt locations around the islands, and money to be made for the local economy, but it needs someone with local connections to make it happen."

"What local connection would that be?"

"Well, there's this prince I know..."

He grinned. "I'm not a prince anymore."

"Okay. There's this former prince I know who seems to have an 'in' with the mayor."

"Is that all? Or is there more to this five year plan?"

"Oh no. I've discovered I'm really quite ambitious. You see, I plan to be a working mum. I think the islands would be the perfect place to raise my children one day."

"And do these hypothetical children have a father?"

"Of course they do. He's this amazingly talented photographer who is single handedly saving the sea turtles of the Caribbean."

He tugged her back into his lap. "And does this paragon have a name?"

She wrapped her legs around his waist. "Now you're just fishing for compliments."

"I want to be sure before I propose that I'm not interfering with some other big plan."

"Shut up and kiss me."

Rik obliged.

@RikWaldburg: @KenzieCole101 Have I told you yet today how much I love you?

Epilogue

@LeeHill: @KenzieCole101 Look at those buns. I could just eat him up.

@KenzieCole101: @LeeHill Hands off, I saw him first.

Kenzie grinned down at the screen of her mobile.

"What's so funny?" Rik asked, tucking his arm through hers.

"Nothing. Just a tweet from Lee." She slid the phone into her tiny sequinned handbag.

"Why are you tweeting him? He's only across the room." He looked across the crowded Orangery to the buffet table. Lee waved back, cheeks dimpling as he grinned.

Kenzie laughed, smiling up at him, and Rik suddenly felt like a million bucks. No, he had a few of those, and this felt way better.

He glanced down the length of the sunlit room where the cast and crew mingled. In another two days they'd be filming right here in this room.

"How much longer do we need to hang around?" he asked, pulling her against him.

"The party's only just started!"

He sighed. "Okay, how about a glass of wine then to pass the time?"

"No thanks."

He frowned. "I made sure they had your favourite white in stock."

She grinned, a flash of mischief in her eyes. "Thank you for your consideration, but unless you have some other idea of how to use it other than drinking..."

The realisation hit him between the eyes. "You're sure?"

Her grin widened. "Turns out that wasn't a stomach bug I picked up in Los Pajaros."

"But there was only that one time we didn't use protection."

"Once is all it takes." She tensed. "You're not unhappy?"

"How could I be unhappy? I'm ecstatic." He swept her off her feet and she laughed.

When he bent his head to kiss her, a voice intruded. "This is the film's meet and greet. Stop making out and come meet someone." Gerry, the likeable teddy bear of a Unit Production Manager.

Rik repressed the urge to throttle him.

"I want you to meet the star of our film, Christian Taylor. Christian, this is our new location liaison Kenzie Cole, and her fiancé Rik Waldburg."

Rik turned. And froze. He scarcely saw the face, or the polite hand outstretched to him. His gaze locked on the pendant hanging on a leather thong around the actor's neck.

"Where did you get that ring?" His body felt as though it had gone into sudden shock, the prickle at the back of his neck electrifying.

Christian looked down, as if he scarcely remembered what he wore. "I found it among my mother's things. She died recently."

Kenzie's grip tightened on his arm. "I'm sorry to hear that. Will you please excuse us?"

She dragged Rik away. His gaze still followed the actor as he turned away to greet someone else.

"What's wrong with you?" she hissed.

"That's the third ring, the missing ring." The odd sensation

187

passed. He looked down at Kenzie. She looked perplexed, clearly not following.

"Some time back in the 1700s, the then Archduke of Westerwald had three rings made for his sons. The Waldburg Rings, they were called. They're the mark of the heirs of Westerwald. I have one, Max has one. The third disappeared shortly before I was born. So how in all that's holy did it end up around the neck of an actor from Hollywood?"

Lightning Source UK Ltd.
Milton Keynes UK
UKHW011825190719
346484UK00001B/61/P

9 780007 559763